GREAT ESCAPES

MOUNT ST. HELENS 1980 FIERY ERUPTION!

GARE THOMPSON

All inquiries should be addressed to:
Barron's Educational Series, Inc.
250 Wireless Boulevard
Hauppauge, New York 11788
www.barronseduc.com

ISBN: 978-1-4380-0972-8

Library of Congress Control Number: 2016962755

Date of Manufacture: April 2017
Manufactured by: M19A19R

Printed in Canada
9 8 7 6 5 4 3 2 1

INTRODUCTION

Alex and Wendy

It's 1980, and thirteen-year-olds Alex Porter and Wendy Adams are best friends. Wendy lives in Portland, Oregon, while Alex's home is a couple hours' drive away in Nighthawk, a very small town located near Mount St. Helens in Washington State. Alex's other best friend is Michael, an older gentleman (he never really admitted his true age, but Alex and Wendy guess he is at least eighty-years-old). The three share their love for Mount St. Helens and nearby Spirit Lake. The eruption of the volcanic mountain, which they nicknamed "Smoky," devastates the area and challenges their friendship as they must learn to work as a team to survive the blast.

Mount St. Helens and the surrounding area has since recovered from that eruption in 1980. However, it remains an active volcano and, as Wendy predicts, Mount St. Helens could erupt again. Today, geologists monitor the mountain striving to predict the next eruption.

The 1980s

The story of Mount St. Helens takes place
in the state of Washington, on the West Coast
of the United States. In 1980, there were no cell
phones, home computers, or laptops; the Internet
was still years away from being developed;
people used land-line telephones or wrote letters
to communicate with friends and relatives.

Also during this decade, Stephen King was a
popular writer of horror stories, and Wendy and
Alex may have secretly read his books under their
bed covers. Blondie was a popular rock band of
the 1980s as well and a favorite of Wendy's.

CHAPTER 1

PACIFIC NORTHWEST 1980

Alex gathered his sketching materials and put them in his backpack. Luckily, February wasn't as cold as usual, so it was the perfect time to be outside drawing his favorite subject—Mount St. Helens, or as his friend Michael called the mountain, "Smoky." The winter weather was mild and the day was sunny, and Alex never tired of drawing Smoky. Like Michael, Smoky had become part of his daily life. Though having a mountain as a best friend might seem odd to most thirteen-year-olds, Alex often found himself chatting with Smoky and referring to the mountain as she, as if Smoky were a real person. Wendy, Alex's human best friend, often said that with Smoky as a "best friend" it explained why Alex was such a lone wolf. His devotion to Smoky sometimes made Wendy jealous. *Well, Wendy will just have to get used to sharing me*, thought Alex. While on his way to his favorite spot, Alex planned to visit Michael, so he had to allow for an extra half hour. He knew Michael would have another interesting story or two about Mount St. Helens to share.

Alex loved the stories that Michael told about Smoky. Most were legends. *I'll have to get Michael to tell Wendy one when she gets here from Portland*, Alex thought. Even though Wendy believed in science and only read nonfiction, she did enjoy legendary tales. And she and Michael got along great, too. Wendy, with her bold red hair, reminded Michael of Lucille Ball, a red-headed comedienne who had starred in the old television series *I Love Lucy*. Alex thought Wendy was funny, but not that funny, though when Alex and Michael had watched an episode of the show, Alex had to agree that Lucille Ball and Wendy did have much in common. Both were impulsive and not all that coordinated and, of course, they each had curly red hair. There was one other difference. Lucille Ball had a sidekick named Ethel on the show, and Alex had no intention of being Wendy's sidekick in wild adventures no matter what Michael said.

Michael had lived in a lodge on the Smoky slopes for over sixty years. During that time, Michael shared what he had learned about camping, for example, with Alex and his family, including ways to stay dry overnight. Alex learned the hard way, waking up one morning in his water-filled tent floating on an inflatable cushion placed under his sleeping bag for comfort. Rainfall isn't usually the main culprit, but water seepage from below often is. Michael advised Alex to pitch his tent on well-drained ground like pine needles and dirt, avoiding shallow depressions where water can quickly accumulate.

But Michael's greatest impression on Alex was relating tales about the mountain, some exaggerated, but always interesting. Living so near the foothills meant that Smoky was Michael's constant companion. Alex's mother worked as a guide for tourists visiting Mount St. Helens, and she had introduced Alex to Michael, knowing that Alex would love his stories as much as she did when she was younger.

Alex glanced at the sparkling rock on his dresser. Michael had given him the rock, which he called "black gold," around seven years ago. Alex treated it more like a jewel, even though at first glance it looked like an ordinary piece of mica. However, to Alex it was very special. The rock was formed from a piece of lava from an eruption of Smoky over 150 years ago. Michael had found it on one of his many hikes. Alex was impressed by the way the rock shone in the sunlight; when lit, it made the rock look as if it had magical qualities, and Alex liked to think it did. However, Alex had to admit, even though he had rubbed the rock frequently when he was little, the rock had never granted Alex a single wish. Alex laughed. Wendy would have his head if he ever admitted that he thought a rock could grant wishes. She was too much of a scientist for that kind of thinking. Still, Alex rubbed the rock when he wanted good luck. *It's my little secret*, he thought.

Alex had brought the rock to his kindergarten class for show and tell. His classmates had not been impressed until Alex shared the story of how Smoky had exploded, breathing ash and fire and spewing lava that flowed down its sides. Once they had heard it was lava rock from that long-ago eruption, his classmates found the rock to be much cooler than they had initially. Some of the kids had thought Alex was making up the volcano part because back then, and even today, the mountain was very peaceful and the perfect place to visit about any time of year. Many of the kids had spent time on Smoky or fishing and boating in Spirit Lake, so Alex's volcano story seemed totally made up. However, Alex's teacher, Mrs. Dooley, confirmed that Mount St. Helens was an active volcano that had erupted about a hundred years ago. Mrs. Dooley was a Native American, a member of the local Cowlitz tribe. She often related stories and interesting facts about all tribes in the region with her class.

Mrs. Dooley and Michael shared a love of the mountain and its legends. She invited Michael to lecture to Alex's class about the history of Mount St. Helens. Michael was a retired history teacher who was used to speaking to students. He chuckled along with the rest of the class when one of Alex's classmates blurted out that there was much less history to learn when Michael was teaching!

Since that classroom appearance, he and Alex had become very close. Some of Alex's young pals thought it was odd that he had a best friend as old as Michael, but Alex didn't care. The two shared a love for the outdoors and for good old Smoky. And no one knew the history of the area better than Michael. Alex quickly sharpened his pencils, carefully placed them in a pocket in his backpack where they wouldn't get broken, and was finally ready. Before leaving, he rubbed his lava rock for luck.

Alex raced down to the kitchen to grab some snacks and water. His father, an architect, was in his home office working on a model of his latest development project. Alex usually loved talking with him about designing buildings, but he questioned his father's new project. The project was the construction of expensive homes around Spirit Lake. Alex and his father had argued about the project, and even though the project was just in the planning stages, Alex was opposed to it. He didn't want any new building to ruin the peaceful wilderness area around his favorite mountain. Alex, usually calm and quiet, had spirited arguments with his father over the project. Alex adamantly opposed any changes to Smoky and Spirit Lake.

His father claimed that the development would not damage the environment, but he couldn't deny that tourists would flock to the area to fish and hike. More vacation homes would only attract more visitors. *So much for solitude*, Alex thought. Unlike many of his friends, Alex preferred being alone. He had no desire to be part of a clique. It was one thing he had in common with Wendy, though he knew she had a circle of friends in Portland. Alex played soccer and ran track, but he preferred being alone to group activities. And since Alex was average in looks and the way he dressed, it was easy for him to disappear in groups. Of course, Wendy teased him about being such a loner, but she understood, too—though he could do without her calling him "Lone Wolf" and howling when she greeted him.

"I'm off to sketch," Alex yelled as he grabbed his jacket and hat, running out the door before his father could stop him. Alex didn't like avoiding his father, but he figured avoidance was better than arguing and spoiling both their days. Besides, Alex knew Michael felt the same way, so the two could vent about the project, and that was much better than Alex debating with his father.

Alex's father watched his son leave and sighed. He looked down at his model homes and shook his head sadly. Alex couldn't be convinced that the development wouldn't ruin Mount St. Helens or Spirit Lake. His father figured Alex was probably stopping at Michael's on his way up the mountain, which would not help settle their disagreement, as Michael was even more opposed to the development than Alex. His father had heard that Michael might even be spearheading a protest of the development. Alex's father hoped his son wouldn't get caught up in Michael's politics; he didn't want to see the split between them grow. In his head, Alex's father increased the number of silver fir and hemlock trees that his company had agreed to plant once the development was completed. Over time, Alex wouldn't even notice that any trees had been removed and be fine with the project. At least, that's how he hoped Alex would react.

As Alex headed toward Michael's lodge, he heard song sparrows chattering away. They blended with the thin, sweet whistles of white-crowned sparrows and the louder, insect-like sounds of Savannah sparrows. Their combined sounds soothed his hurt feelings over the development. *I'll ask Michael to tell me what life* on Mount St. Helens was like in "the old days," Alex thought, and that way he could avoid thinking about the development. There was no sense in ruining a perfect day. *I should have made a wish when I rubbed the rock. I could have wished all my troubles away.* The sunshine and slight breeze on his face made Alex smile. *Maybe the rock was magical.* In his head, Alex could hear Wendy shout, "No way! It's just a piece of lava. Interesting, yes; magical, no."

There were just enough white, fluffy clouds in the blue sky, so the sun cast gentle shadows of the evergreen trees. In Alex's mind, the evergreens were giants standing guard over the mountain. They loomed there, protecting Smoky. Alex hoped he remembered the image when he settled into his special spot, as it would make a cool drawing, almost like a cartoon. Alex saw Michael bundled up—even though it wasn't that cold—sitting in his weathered white rocker, so Alex waved. Michael waved back. Alex picked up his pace and soon was standing on Michael's porch.

"Hey, Van Gogh, how goes it today?" Michael asked, and Alex laughed at his nickname. Of course, he wasn't a master artist like Vincent Van Gogh, but it was neat that Michael recognized his talent. He liked Michael's nickname much better than Wendy's, plus Michael didn't howl at him.

"Fine," Alex replied. "I just wanted to pop in and say hello before I head up to my spot. I'm thinking it's a perfect day for sketching."

Michael looked up at the sky. "You're right about that, though I must admit my bones do ache a little."

Alex stifled a laugh since, at Michael's age, his bones always seemed to be aching. (No one was quite sure how old Michael was, as his age changed depending on the story he was telling, but he was close to eighty or even a little older.) Alex waited for Michael to tell him how his sore bones could predict the weather, and sure enough he did.

"Probably going to rain later, given how my right knee is twitching," Michael commented.

"Though I'm wondering if Smoky is as calm as she looks. My bones have been hurting lately, and that means more than rain."

Alex looked up at Smoky. "She looks pretty peaceful to me," he replied. Recently, Michael kept saying that Mount St. Helens was an active volcano, not a dormant one. However, nothing had happened in the last one hundred years, so Alex was pretty sure it was just Michael's age that caused his knee to twitch. Besides, his mother had talked to the local geologists, and though they did agree with Michael that Mount St. Helens was an active volcano, no one was predicting an eruption—except, of course, Wendy, whose new obsession was volcanoes. But since she lived a distant fifty miles away in Portland, her predictions of an eruption were just wishful thinking. *Sorry, Wendy, but I think you need a new obsession,* Alex thought. Still, Michael's next comment startled Alex.

"Do you hear that?" Michael asked. Alex frowned. He didn't hear anything. Maybe Michael was having an off day.

"I don't hear anything," he answered. Michael looked up at the sky. He had a quizzical look on his wrinkled face. Michael stood up, causing his rocker to fly backwards, and peered at the sky.

"Look," Michael pointed up. Alex stared skyward, but he didn't notice anything except white clouds and patches of blue sky.

"Am I missing something?" Alex asked. "I don't hear anything, and I don't see anything but a beautiful sky." Alex tried to laugh, but Michael shook his head and frowned.

"That's exactly right," Michael said. "Silence. Where are the birds? The nighthawks, the blackbirds?" The question puzzled Alex, but even stranger was that Michael was right. On his way to Michael's, the birds were singing, but now it was strangely silent. Suddenly, Mount St. Helens seemed spooky, much like when all goes quiet in a horror movie and then suddenly the villain appears. *I take it back Wendy; maybe your obsession is not so crazy after all*, he thought. Alex took a deep breath. Still, he wasn't scared of an eruption—at least that's what he told himself.

"I guess they flew away," Alex shrugged his shoulders.

Michael shook his head in reply. "It's not a good sign with no birds communicating. They always leave or go silent when there is some kind of danger," Alex didn't like the concern on Michael's face, so he tried to make light of the subject.

"I think your own stories about Mount St. Helens are getting to you," Alex said. "My mom talked with the geologists. We're not in any danger. It's just your bones aching because of your age. Trust me; all is fine." Alex laughed, but Michael didn't join in.

"Depends on your definition of fine," Michael replied ominously. "I think more than precipitation is coming, and I don't mean snow. I think the legend about Smoky is finally going to come true."

CHAPTER 2

"Which legend is that?" Alex asked. Michael had told him so many yarns that Alex had a hard time keeping them straight. But he didn't even mind when Michael repeated himself because Michael always changed his story from the time before.

"Oh, you know. The one about the two warriors." Alex didn't remember this one. Besides, it was clear that Michael was ready to tell him a tale, so Alex settled back on the porch railing to enjoy it. He'd still have plenty of time to sketch. And the legend might give him some ideas for his drawings.

"Let's hear it," Alex smiled.

The storyteller in Michael took over. He cleared his throat and began, his voice deep and rich. "Well, long, long ago, according to old Indian tales, a powerful chief lived here with his two sons. And in the village lived this beautiful princess."

Alex rolled his eyes. *A romance, really?* But Michael ignored Alex's reaction and kept going. "Each one wanted her for his wife, so of course, the two battled for her. Now their fighting made the princess feel very important, and she was truly flattered by their love for her. However, she did not want to choose between the two warriors. She did not want the brothers to remain enemies. So, she would not choose one over the other. The princess even tried to make peace between the young, lovesick men.

"However, the princess couldn't prevent them from battling, which became fiercer over time. Finally, the Great Spirit became aware of the conflict from the complaints of his people. He became angry that the warriors were destroying the peaceful ways. He was also upset with the princess for not making a choice. Finally, the Great Spirit acted. He covered all three of them in stone, and they became separate mountains." Michael paused, his voice returning to normal, "Guess which mountain the princess is?"

Alex immediately knew the answer, as Michael always referred to the mountain as his "girl." He blurted out, "Smoky!"

"That's right," Michael replied. His voice returned to the mellow tones of a storyteller. "Now most of the time the princess sleeps peacefully, but every one hundred years or so, she wakes up. And when that happens, she is angry. In fact, she gets so enraged that she blows her top off." Michael clapped his hands as he yelled, "BOOM!," imitating Smoky erupting. Alex jumped back. Michael, with his eyes bright and shiny, grinned at Alex who grinned right back. *Wendy would love that tale*, he thought. A legend that explains volcanoes. Of course, she'd reject the romance part and then explain in excruciating detail how volcanoes really worked. Still, it was a good tale. Alex looked around. *Of course, it isn't true, it's just a legend.*

"I think 'my girl' is waking up," Michael said. Alex knew that Michael wasn't superstitious, but he didn't think Michael's knees or his stories were reliable predictors of a volcano eruption. Just as Alex was about to respond, he heard the familiar drumming sound of Northern Flicker woodpeckers in nearby fir trees. "See, the birds are back," Alex said. *Case closed.*

"Maybe, but something made them go away," Michael mumbled. "Remember, the Native Americans didn't call it 'Smoke Mountain' for nothing."

Without thinking, Alex nodded. Michael was not about to change his mind or be persuaded that Smoky was not going to erupt. So Alex said he'd be on his way. He almost added, "Before Mount St. Helens erupts," but he didn't want to mock Michael. "I'm off then," Alex said as he started up the path.

"Be careful," Michael yelled as he waved. "I know something is not right," he muttered as he settled back into his rocker. "Mark my words." Once seated, Michael pulled out his binoculars that he kept by the rocker. "Still, not a bird way high in the sky," Michael said to himself. "Something is up. I don't like this one bit, but no matter what happens, you're not getting rid of me, 'girl.' I'm here to stay."

As he reached the summit on the path, Alex looked back down at Michael on the porch. Michael was peering through his binoculars, so Alex waved one more time. Michael also gestured, put away the binoculars, and then sat there rocking away. In school, Alex's class was studying the ancient Greeks and Romans, and Michael's rocking and making predictions reminded Alex of the description of the Greek oracles. *They couldn't really foretell the future either*, Alex thought as he turned onto his secret path.

Alex was panting by the time he reached his destination. The trail was rocky and a hard climb, which was why very few people ever took it, plus the air became thinner the farther up one climbed. Most people, including his mother, preferred the paths that wound up around the mountain and were easier to walk. Still, it was a shorter route to the summit area where Alex could get a clear view of the mountaintop. Michael had shown Alex the shortcut. Alex was intrigued by the notion of this secret path, and he couldn't wait to share it with Wendy on her next visit. Plus, it would be fun to watch her try to talk and walk at the same time.

Crawling under his favorite evergreen tree, Alex felt safe and secure. The tree had long branches that formed a roof over a space, making it a perfect room for Alex. The branches kept out the cold, and inside was warm; even the ground under the branch was dry, as the snow in this area had melted and the fallen evergreen needles worked like a cushion. Alex was not very tall, so his space was nice and snug. He was hidden if anyone should be on the path, yet he could peer through the branches. And, since he was on the far side of the mountain, he still had a panoramic view of the Mount St.

Helens summit. As the ads in tourist brochures proclaimed, the scenery was spectacular.

Alex knew Smoky so well that he could really draw her from any angle. All he had to do was close his eyes, and she appeared, but he loved hiking the mountain and his special spot. Relaxed and content, Alex got out his drawing pad and pencils. He blew on his cold hands to limber them up. *Time to get to work*, he thought.

Alex quickly sketched the shape of his favorite mountain. First, he drew a pyramid shape. Then he began slowly filling in the details. Alex never tired of filling in the snow-capped peak and the different shades of blue. Even though it had been a mild winter, the fallen snow still lingered on the ground at higher elevations. Spring seemed far off, rather than just around the corner. Alex gradually added in the forest of evergreens that framed the mountain. Smoky reminded Alex of the painting he had seen of Mount Fuji in Japan. Later, he would use his oils to create different shades of white so the mountain would seem to glow. Then he would shade the evergreens so they looked like soldiers guarding the mountain.

Maybe he'd give them a warrior feel like the young men in the legend Michael had told. *No, I think I'll make them look like Samurai*, Alex thought. He wanted to keep with the Japanese feeling and the resemblance to Mount Fuji. Smiling, he was glad he remembered the idea of the evergreens being guards. It would make his drawing different from the hundreds of postcard images of Mount St. Helens that the tourists bought in the gift shops at Spirit Lake. Though there was nothing wrong with the postcards, Alex wanted his drawing to be unique—or, as Wendy would say, "Special." Soon Alex was lost in his drawing, and the time flew by.

Alex looked forward to sharing the drawing with his father, who had introduced him to Japanese art. However, thoughts of his father made the development loom up before Alex's eyes, and he remembered the heated words he and his father had exchanged. Alex sighed and regretted the incident, but he knew he couldn't take them back. He turned his attention back to his drawing, blocking out those thoughts. Alex wished he and his father could come to an agreement about the development, but now was not the time to think about that. Alex deftly gave some of the evergreen branches the feel of swords. *Nice to meet you, Honorable Evergreen,* Alex thought.

Once his sketch was finished, Alex put away his pad and pencils and sat back to soak in the serenity. While Alex loved sketching, his favorite part of the day was when he just sat there and let the peace and quiet wash over him. His concerns about his father and the development drifted away. Alex pictured them floating up into the sky and then being chased away by the birds.

Alex wondered what his friend Wendy was doing. She was going to visit, and he knew she'd want to explore Smoky with him. Hiking the mountain was one of their favorite pastimes, even if Wendy did complain (loudly) about all the hiking. Wendy preferred books and reading to most physical activities. Alex smiled. He did enjoy aggravating her by dashing way ahead up the path, though her heavy breathing and complaining often made him slow to a crawl. They'd probably stop to see Michael, too. Wendy would have taken Michael's warnings seriously. With Wendy's latest obsession with volcanoes, she was convinced that Mount St. Helens was going to erupt any day now. Alex shook his head. The real reason Wendy was convinced Smoky would blow her top was because she was the only "active" volcano that was near enough for Wendy to visit and observe. She claimed Smoky was the perfect place for her to practice being a volcanologist.

The air grew colder and Alex felt the chill, so he decided to return home. Maybe there was a letter from Wendy awaiting him. During the trip back, Alex whistled and the birds whistled back. He also spotted some squirrels racing around trees. The animals had not abandoned Smoky. *Nothing to worry about,* he thought. *Michael, the oracle, is wrong.*

CHAPTER 3

Upon returning home, Alex pulled off his jacket, shoved his hat into the sleeve, and hung it up on the hook in the hallway. He was about to announce his presence when his father suddenly appeared.

"Making much progress on your sketching?" Alex waited a moment before replying. His father was obviously trying to make peace, and after Alex's great day, he was open to it. Besides, Alex knew his father was genuinely interested in his drawing, so Alex shared his sketch with him.

"Alex, this is really strong. Are you going to paint it in oils or use your pastels?" his father asked.

"I think I'll try oils for a layered look," Alex replied. He wasn't comfortable with oils, as he had just started seriously using them, but he trusted his gut and oils seemed to be the answer if he wanted to get the shading, layers, and the feel of Japanese art.

"Well, it'll be impressive. It reminds me of a Japanese print," his father said.

Alex smiled. "That's what I was going for."

"You pulled it off," Alex's mother said as she came into the hall from the kitchen. She had returned from work but was still wearing her tour guide uniform. She peeked at the drawing over Alex's shoulder. "Nice work, Van Gogh." His mother had picked up Michael's nickname.

"Thanks," Alex murmured as a lock of hair fell over his eyes. "I'm going to put it away."

Alex started for his room, but his father grabbed his arm. "I think you might want to take this." He handed Alex a letter.

"Gee, I wonder who it's from?" his mother smiled. Alex's mom and Mrs. Adams had been best friends since college, and the two were pleased that their children got along so well. Whenever Wendy and Alex said that they were just friends, maybe best friends, the two mothers would look at each other and nod. In fact, one night when Wendy was visiting, they discussed how the two were so different. It was true; Wendy could be impulsive and unfocused, while Alex was very quiet and more attentive. Alex's mom had mentioned about how opposites attract. Their differences occasionally upset both Alex and Wendy, but they still enjoyed each other's company. *Even if Wendy was a little obsessive,* Alex chuckled to himself. And Wendy claimed Alex was way too serious and too much the lone wolf. Alex had to agree with her description, but he really wished she would stop howling when she greeted him. Hopefully she'd stick to the Van Gogh nickname, though Alex was sure that Wendy would come up with some shtick, like pretending to paint him or something. *Oh well, that was Wendy being Wendy.*

Alex placed his drawing carefully on the desk in his room. Alex had the canvas stretched and he was ready to begin painting tomorrow. He sat on his bed, got out his water and snacks, and ripped open Wendy's letter. Once Wendy started lecturing about her fascination with volcanoes, she was like a runaway train engine careening around the tracks. Still, Alex looked forward to hearing from her, and he settled in to read her missive (a new word he'd picked up from Michael). In his head, Alex replied and reacted to Wendy's letters.

Hey, Lone Wolf—oh wait, or are you Van Gogh today, or have you switched to Monet? Go Impressionism!!!

∘◯◯ Really, Wendy, one nickname is bad enough.

I don't know if I told you, but we're studying Mount Vesuvius as part of our Earth Science lessons.

∘◯◯ You've told me about five hundred times.

It's pretty amazing. Vesuvius is the only active volcano on mainland Europe. Did you know it overlooks the bay and the city of Naples?

I'm sure you know it's famous for its eruption in 79 A.D.

∘◯◯ I do know.

The eruption destroyed the cities of Pompeii and Herculaneum. But I bet you don't know that its last significant eruption was in 1944, so you can see, just like Mount St. Helens, it's an ACTIVE volcano!!!!!!

∘◯◯ The only thing erupting is either your pen from the number of exclamation points or your brain from too many volcano facts.

That means it could go off at any time. However, geologists aren't sure when the next eruption could occur. That's EXACTLY the same as Mount St. Helens—or, as you and Michael call it, Smoky. And she will live up to her name! By the way, I refuse to call Smoky "her." Mountains do not have a gender. No matter how many legends Michael tells, and I do like his legends, mountains do NOT really have personalities. Get it or be square!!!!

Back to Vesuvius. There have been at least 18 eruptions in the last 17,000 years. MAJOR ONES!!!!!!!!! The one in 79 A.D. killed about 16,000 people. That's sad, but what's cool is they suffocated and the ash covered them, so their bodies were preserved. Then archaeologists found them. I mean it's not cool that they suffocated, but it is neat that the dead bodies were preserved. Some of the people have expressions on their faces, so it's almost like you know what they were thinking. When I see you this weekend, I'll bring a book I have on Pompeii. You may want to do some sketches from the photos.

○◯◯ Ugh, not really. Kind of ghoulish, Wendy.

Although I have to admit being curious.

In 1631, Vesuvius had steady eruptions, with a flow of lava. Then, ash and mud spewed into the sky. It was kind of like a reminder that the volcano—notice no pronoun—was active. Volcanoes are so destructive, but they are also amazing. You know that like, after a fire, the area rebuilds itself. Animals return, plants begin to thrive, and the land rejuvenates itself. Now, that is cool!!!!!!!!!!!!!!

During the 1944 eruption of Vesuvius, planes in the area were grounded and even soldiers had to be evacuated. Don't worry!!!! Helicopters could fly into the area to rescue victims. I checked with some local pilots. Your mom can probably verify that.

○○○ I will ask her.

Who knew that a volcano proved to be an enemy in World War II? Not as bad as that horrible guy in charge, Benito Mussolini, but still bad.

Of course, Pliny the Younger, a Roman historian, described the event in 79 A.D. It's like the most famous eyewitness account of a volcano in history. Of course, my report on Mount St. Helens will be better!!!!!!!

The poor guy's uncle was one of the thousands who died in Pompeii. Here's his description. It's fascinating!!!!!!

"On 24 August, in the early afternoon, my mother drew my uncle's attention to a cloud of unusual size and appearance. Its general appearance can be best expressed as being like an umbrella pine, for it rose to a great height on a sort of trunk and then split off into branches, I imagine because it was thrust upwards

32

by the first blast and then left unsupported as the pressure subsided, or else it was borne down by its own weight so that it spread out and gradually dispersed. Sometimes it looked white, sometimes blotched and dirty, according to the amount of soil and ashes it carried with it."

I wonder if Smoky will look like a pine tree when it erupts!!!!!!!

○◯◯ Gee, Wendy, way to kill my love of evergreens.

Anyway, not much else is new. I am being forced to pick a sport, so I settled on indoor track. Can you picture me running? I can't.

○◯◯ Makes two of us.

So, I'm trying to run every day. Luckily, this winter is mild, otherwise, I'd be toast—HAHA, not really, more like a frozen waffle!!! I'd rather be spotting volcanoes, but what can I say? See you soon. Can't wait to hike your favorite mountain. It had better not erupt until I get there!!!!!!!!!!!! Just kidding...well, sort of... Here's howling at you!!!!

Your pal,

Wendy

I'm not like you, Van Gogh, but you get the idea!!!!!!!!!!!!!!!!!!!!!!!!!

Alex added it to the pile of Wendy's letters.
They were like a mini-mountain. Alex wasn't
sure how he felt about Wendy's new fascination.
He understood it and in some ways thought it
was cool, but on the other hand, the constant
reminder that Smoky might blow drove Alex
a little crazy. As far as Alex was concerned,
Smoky was fast asleep and not going to erupt,
no matter what Wendy and Michael thought.
Besides, most predictions were only right half

the time, at least that's what Alex hoped. Alex's mother called Alex down to dinner.

"Coming," he replied, jumping off his bed to go to the kitchen.

CHAPTER 4

During dinner, Alex's mother asked, "So what's new with my favorite redhead?"

Alex replied, "Well, Wendy's really into volcanoes."

Alex's mother shook her head. She was used to Wendy changing obsessions. "I suppose exploring visible volcanoes make more sense than invisible ghosts."

Last year, Wendy was hooked on ghosts and was convinced that one lived in a lodge near Michael's lodge. It took four trips to the deserted place at all times of the day and night before Wendy dropped her theory that a ghost lived there. Michael encouraged her by insisting the lodge was haunted. In fact, he claimed the former owners had died during a storm atop Mount St. Helens. However, Wendy had searched through old newspapers at the library and had not found any stories that matched Michael's. Alex had reminded Wendy that Michael was known for his tall tales. Still, both had loved the story.

Since Alex had no desire to discuss whether Smoky might erupt, he changed the subject and asked, "So how was your day, Mom? Anything new to report on Mount St. Helens?"

Alex knew his mother had spent some time with the geologists that were watching the mountain, and Wendy would grill the family once she was here, so Alex hoped to gather all the information he could and be ready to answer Wendy's questions.

"Oh, just the usual. Families who were hiking the mountain were either overdressed or underdressed, and kids kept asking questions about Mount St. Helens. Someone was wearing fingerless gloves. We should get you a pair. They'd be perfect for you when you sketch."

"Sounds good," Alex commented, though the idea seemed a little weird.

His mother continued, "Luckily, one of the geologists, David Johnston, was with me when those questions came up." Alex's mother laughed. "However, he reminds me of Wendy. Volcanoes are his specialty."

Alex laughed. "You mean he's obsessed too!"

His mother smiled. "So, he ended up lecturing on how a volcano can lie dormant for over a hundred years and then suddenly explode. He explained that they have been monitoring Mount St. Helens, as there seems to be activity in the mountain. His explanation of an eruption being caused by the movement of tectonic plates under the Earth's crust is fascinating. Even though I think the kids may have regretted asking him a question, I learned a lot. Of course, it also caused some families to bolt down the mountain, to escape the 'active' volcano."

"What's his take on Mount St. Helens? Is she ready to blow?" Alex's father asked.

"Well, according to David's measurements and information that he and the other geologists have gathered, the mountain is definitely alive. He's not sure what kind of eruption might happen or when, but he's positive one will occur. No one, however, can predict an exact date. It's sort of like a hurricane. It's all up to Mother Nature. David did share some history of past eruptions, and if the next one is like the eruption that happened over one hundred years ago, we'd have to evacuate the area quickly."

Alex took a sip of his milk. "We'd have to convince Michael to leave." He realized that might be a problem because Michael repeated that if his "girl" erupted, he wasn't leaving his home. "Wendy raised the possibility that helicopters could fly in for rescues. Can they?"

"Yes, a rescue helicopter might be an option," Alex's father nodded in agreement. The idea that helicopters could fly in and out made

Alex feel better about rescuing Michael at the time of an eruption. "And don't worry; I'm sure we could convince Michael to leave," his father said. His mother smiled at Alex's father and continued, reassuring Alex.

"Besides, it's not definite that Mount St. Helens will erupt. Remember, the tectonic plates move all the time, and there are daily earthquakes even if we can't feel them on the Earth's surface. Plus, no one can predict when a volcano will erupt. However, there is historical evidence that active volcanoes erupt every 100 years. So according to that theory, Mount St. Helens is bound to erupt. We must be prepared in case of such an emergency." Mrs. Porter was calm as if she were discussing plans for a family vacation.

"Wendy will be at the top of her game when she gets here," Alex sighed. Wendy would love to lecture him on making plans for any possible evacuation. Maybe he should have her practice racing up and down the mountain. That would fix her. Being out of breath would be about the only way to stop her from talking.

"You know, about 2,000 years ago, a man living in China invented a simple device that recorded movement of the Earth," Alex's father said. "You and Wendy should do some research on it. Maybe you could build one."

Alex stared at his father. *Where did that come from?* Alex wondered.

His father continued, "And there's a Turkish painting from 9,000 years ago that depicts an exploding volcano. At least that's what some scientists think. Wendy might be interested in that, too."

"Wow, you're the go-to parent about anything volcano!" Alex replied.

Alex's father laughed. "Yes, your parents are all-knowing, like the Wizard of Oz."

"Can we change the subject?" Alex asked. "I'll get enough volcano talk when Wendy is here." Alex tried to think of a subject to chat about, like the movie he had recently seen, *Mad Max*. But before he could speak, his father jumped into the conversation.

41

"Well, my company presents our development model to the planning board next week. We're hoping for a quick approval." Alex remained silent, not wanting to spark a debate about a plan he opposed.

"How do you think the vote will go?" Alex's mother asked. Alex knew she didn't approve of the development either. She loved Spirit Lake "as is," but also wanted to support her husband. Alex, on the other hand, voiced his disapproval of the project.

"So far, it looks like it should get approved. There are a couple of members who have questions about the size and impact on Spirit Lake, but I think we've got the right answers for them. The impact on Spirit Lake will be minimal, and the development will create construction jobs and also a steady source of future employment with retail shops opening to cater to the incoming residents and tourists the development would attract."

"Just what we need," Alex muttered sarcastically. Alex's father immediately responded. "Alex, the plan is well thought out and is environmentally sound."

"OK, you two, no bickering at the table. Let's finish our meal in peace," Alex's mother said. Alex shoved some mashed potatoes in his mouth to keep from making another comment. Alex's mother hated being referee, and she definitely did not want the two fighting. Everyone finished the meal in strained silence. Alex excused himself as soon as his plate was clean, took his dish to the kitchen, and then went up to his room. He pulled out the dog-eared copy of H.D. Thoreau's *Walden* that Michael had given him. Communing with Thoreau was much better than arguing with his father. Alex still couldn't believe that after all the hikes and time they had spent together on Mount St. Helens, his father could plan to build a development there and spoil his favorite place on Earth. *That really blew, no pun intended.*

His parents' voices drifted up to his room. His mother was telling his father that Alex still loved him, and his father said he knew, but he wished Alex would at least listen to him. What would happen if his father found out that Alex was thinking of joining those who were going to protest the development if the planning board gave his father's company the green light to proceed? *Well, I'll cross that bridge when I come to it,* Alex thought. He escaped to the woods around Walden Pond and the kind of life he wanted to live—alone with nothing but nature. *Smoky erupting could solve the development problem. No, I wouldn't want that.* Soon Alex and Thoreau were foraging in the woods for nuts, berries, and mushrooms, at peace with nature and the world.

CHAPTER 5

Alex and his mother drove to the bus station in Nighthawk to pick up Wendy. She barreled off the bus and ran over to them. "Wow, you look great, Aunt Jenny!" Wendy exclaimed as she hugged Alex's mother. She wasn't her real aunt, of course, but Wendy treated her like a blood relative. She then turned to Alex and howled again, reminding him of his "Lone Wolf" identity. Alex wondered if Wendy ever did anything without exclamation points. Wendy laughed. Her bright red hair shone in the sunlight. Today, it was in pigtails. She resembled the kid's book heroine, Pippi Longstocking, though Alex wouldn't dare tell Wendy that.

Ah, Wendy, you're like a breath of fresh air," Alex's mother said.

More like a tornado, Alex thought.

Mrs. Porter drove the three back to their house. "Make yourself at home, Wendy," Alex said touting her backpack. "You're only here for one night; why is your backpack so heavy? Barbells?" Alex dropped her backpack on the hallway floor.

"My books. Remember, I brought the one on Pompeii just for you, Van Gogh," Wendy loped off to the guest room. "Oh, bellhop, bring my backpack up, PULEEZE."

Alex laughed. "I expect a big tip."

"Your tip is that Mount St. Helens is going to blow, so be careful," Wendy said.

"Gee, thanks. You can keep that tip to yourself," Alex replied. He looked upset, so Wendy knew not to press him on Smoky.

"Are you ready to go hiking?" Alex asked. He planned that they take his secret path. *Let's see how cheery she is then.*

"Of course," Wendy replied. Alex almost felt guilty about his plan. The key word was *almost*. Wendy took her backpack into the kitchen and then came out. Alex hoped she had unloaded all of her books; otherwise, she'd constantly moan about how heavy it was. Alex had no intention of lugging around her backpack.

Before the two departed, Alex's mother reminded them to take a supply of water. Alex and Wendy looked at each other and laughed. Alex's mother was always telling them to bring water or some other item with them. "You must hydrate," she was fond of saying. Alex filled a canteen and the two finally left.

Michael lived much closer to Smoky than Alex did; it was a pleasant trip to the mountain. Wendy, of course, chattered the whole way. *She's like a magpie,* Alex thought, *except she collects facts instead of shiny objects.* Wendy kept adjusting her backpack as they walked, but she never complained. Alex figured she had left the books behind after all. Or maybe her steady stream of conversation distracted her.

First, Wendy told Alex what was happening at school. Neither Alex nor Wendy really cared for middle school, as it was so different from elementary school. Having different teachers for each subject was strange and a big adjustment from relying on just one teacher. Wendy, however, loved her science class and her teacher, Miss Simons. "How cool is it to have a woman teacher for science?" Wendy asked for the hundredth time.

"Gee, Wendy, I don't know, how cool is it?" Alex asked sarcastically.

"No need to be such a dweeb," Wendy retorted. "It was a *rhetorical* question. I wasn't expecting an answer. How's your painting going? Any masterpieces?" Wendy pretended not to care, but she was really impressed with Alex's work. Wendy recognized his artistic talent, though sometimes she had no clue what his abstract pictures meant.

"Yeah, I'm working on one that has a Japanese feel to it. It's cool." Alex didn't really like to talk about his paintings until they were finished, so he quickly changed the subject. "Should we stop and see Michael?"

"Sure, why not?" Wendy replied. The two hiked to Michael's, enjoying the pleasant scent of the evergreens and the musical symphony of the birds, while trying to spot an elk or a deer. They didn't find one but had fun searching. They reached Michael's lodge and found him in his favorite rocker on the porch. Seeing Michael in the rocker made Alex wonder if Michael slept there, as he seemed to be glued to it most days.

Alex hoped Michael wouldn't share his theory about Smoky erupting with Wendy. That would mean an hour's lost time for sure. Once Wendy started talking about volcanoes, she could go on forever, and Michael often enjoyed egging Wendy on and testing her science knowledge. Alex wished he'd brought his sketchbook.

"Well, if it isn't Van Gogh and my favorite redhead. How are you, Miss Wendy?" Michael stood and bowed to Wendy.

Wendy pretended to curtsy back. "Why, I'm just peachy, sir. Thank you for asking." She used some sort of southern accent that made all three burst out laughing. "Guess I have to work on my accent," Wendy giggled.

"You got that right," Alex replied shaking his head.

Michael and Wendy often acted as if they were characters from a book. It was the one really goofy thing the scientist Wendy did. Alex thought it was odd, but hey, if it made them happy, who was he to judge? The three chatted about the weather, the birds and animals Michael had spotted with his binoculars, and everything except volcanoes. Alex was a happy camper. Michael agreed to hike with them, and without thinking, Alex told Michael to take some water.

Wendy rolled her eyes and said, "Boy Scout Alex, ready and able."

Alex held back on responding to that tease.

The climb up Smoky was leisurely, and the three made several stops on their way to the summit. The forest odors, the refreshing breeze, and the cloudless sky combined for the perfect hike. Michael pointed out some old conifer trees that had grown larger since the last eruption decades earlier. Wendy went on about how good volcanic ash was for the soil. Alex spaced out and admired the view—one he never got tired of.

Wendy told Michael, "He's painting pictures in his head."

Michael laughed. "That's the artist in him. The same way you observe your surroundings— that's the scientist in you."

Wendy beamed. Although Michael never really discussed his background, Wendy had learned that Michael was a retired history teacher, who was highly regarded in his field. When she had told Alex, he had simply groaned. In all his contacts with Michael, his past had never come up. Leave it to Wendy to uncover it; she was the queen of research.

"Too bad we didn't plan for a picnic," Michael said when they reached their destination.

Wendy opened her backpack, and like a cat that swallowed the canary, she pulled out sandwiches. She ribbed Alex, "See, I can be prepared too." The three ate their chicken salad sandwiches, enjoying their surroundings. Once they finished, they cleaned up but weren't yet ready to start back. "How about a tale, Michael?" Alex asked. Michael nodded and began.

"Once upon a time…" He waited for the two to groan, and on cue they did just that. Michael laughed and started over. "Long, long ago, when Smoke Mountain was filled with children and animals, an eruption happened." Wendy sat up and Alex frowned.

Michael continued, "The eruption destroyed all the animals that lived on Smoke Mountain. The children had tried to save them but had been forced to hide in the safety of caves. The children were spared. Still, it was said that the animals returned to haunt the mountain but in grotesque forms. Fish had developed goat heads. Frogs suddenly had sharp spines. All of these strange creatures lived in Spirit Lake, so the adults stopped fishing there. The children never saw any of these creatures so weren't afraid to swim or fish there. It has been said that the children were pure of heart and did not believe in such nonsense."

Michael looked over at Wendy and Alex. Alex was drawing pictures of these animals in his head, while Wendy was debating whether those creatures ever existed in the first place. Alex waited for Wendy to launch into a lecture on a possible eruption, but she didn't.

"Let's head back," Alex ordered. For once, Michael and Wendy agreed. The three returned to Michael's home. Alex and Wendy said good-bye to Michael and then started for Alex's house.

"That was a weird tale, and not weird in a good way," Wendy said.

"Yeah, it was strange. Though the creatures did give me some ideas for paintings. It would be fun to create them and have them swimming in Spirit Lake," Alex replied.

"You realize they couldn't have existed, right?" Wendy said. "I mean, no animals would have those kinds of adaptations. Adaptations happen for survival." Alex rolled his eyes.

"Duh, yeah, I know. It's just a story," Alex replied. The two completed the rest of their journey in silence.

During dinner later that day, they chatted about school, and Wendy remarked she wanted to return to the mountain to take some photos the next day. Alex agreed. The weather was perfect and Wendy got some great shots of Smoky and Spirit Lake. Alex began his sketches of the lake. The two made plans for Wendy to return soon for a whole weekend. By the time Wendy boarded the bus for home, she was so tired that she slept the whole way. Alex went to bed early, too, and both of them had odd dreams about Smoky and the weird animals who once may have lived there but probably didn't.

CHAPTER 6

Dear Alex,

This is a quick note I want to get in the mail before I arrive this coming weekend.

○○○ **Brevity, thy name is not Wendy.**

Anyway, I've been doing more research on Mount St. Helens... I will have a list of questions for the geologists when I get there. Michael's talk about eruptions has set me off—HAHA joke, get it?

○○○ **Got it!**

Here's what I've learned. Mount St. Helens is a composite volcano, or stratovolcano. That means it is steep-sided, and the cones are symmetrical and constructed of alternating layers of lava flows, ash, and other volcanic debris. Isn't that cool?

○○○ **If you say so, Wendy. No clue what you are talking about.**

The local Native Americans and early settlers witnessed the occasional violent eruptions. It was active from around 1831 to 1857. There are reports from people about the "smoking mountain" erupting. However, no big eruptions occurred, which is why I think that if it does erupt now, it will be a really, really big bang!!!!!!!!!!!!!

ₒ◯◯ I hope not, Wendy!!!!!!!!!!

I think that the people there should be warned. I mean, the mountain and Spirit Lake attract a lot of tourists, and they probably don't know the history of Mount St. Helens. This puts them in potential danger. Most people think the only "active" volcanoes are in Hawaii or Alaska. That is just WRONG!!!!!!!!!!!

You may think I'm just crazy, but I'm not, Alex—trust me. The possible eruption is SERIOUS STUFF. A group of scientists have been studying Mount St. Helens since the 1950s. The Cascade mountain range extends from southern Canada down to California, a distance of about 700 miles. The scientists think that even though your favorite mountain is the youngest of the major Cascade volcanoes, it is the most active, and they are really concerned about its possible eruptions. In fact, one scientist who was referring to the Cascade chain in an article from May 1968 that I dug up said that he was "especially worried about snow-covered Mount St. Helens."

o◯◯ But Wendy, nothing has happened.

AND two other scientists concluded that Mount St. Helens is very active and ready to erupt!!!!!!!!!!!!!!!!!!!!!!!!!!!!!!!!!!!! So it's not just me.

The first sign will be a series of small earthquakes, so if that happens, RUN!!!!! By the way, did you know that the ancient Chinese developed an earthquake machine? They were able to predict earthquakes. How cool is that?

o◯◯ I do know. Thanks, Dad.

BUT, no one has invented a machine to predict volcano eruptions!!!!!!!!!

Can't wait to see you. Yours in eruptions—HAHA—the future volcanologist, Wendy

CHAPTER 7

Alex awoke to another morning of sunshine. It was hard to believe it was even winter. Looking out his window, Alex could just make out the crystal-clear waters of Spirit Lake, and even though it was still early—well, early for a Saturday—Alex could see a few fishermen on the lake. *Yes, it's going to be a good day,* he thought. *There's no way Mount St. Helens is erupting. Sorry, Wendy.* Alex threw on his favorite T-shirt, a sweatshirt, and a pair of hiking pants. He was due at Michael's by 9:30, and the two were going to take a leisurely hike, though Michael's idea of leisurely was not the same as other people's—even though Michael used a walking stick (the top was a carved yellow goldfinch, the state bird of Washington). Alex heard his parents in the kitchen and headed downstairs.

"Morning, son," greeted Alex's father in between bites of raisin toast. Alex helped himself to a bowl of cornflakes and milk.

"Want some nuts and raisins on your cereal?" his mother asked.

Alex nodded, and his mother pushed a bowl toward Alex. "They will give you more energy for your hike."

"How'd you know I was going for a hike?" Sometimes, it seemed his mother could tell the future.

His mother laughed and pointed to his hiking pants and heavy socks. "I'm not Sherlock Holmes, but it was an astute deduction. All that's missing are your gloves and jacket."

"Oh, right," Alex muttered as he finished his cereal.

"Take it easy, sport; the mountain isn't going anywhere," his father said as he patted Alex's arm.

"I know, Dad," said Alex. He saw his father stiffen, so he tried to lighten his tone. "But you know how Michael is about being late."

His father smiled. "True. Have a safe hike. And say hello to Michael for me."

Alex almost asked his father to join them but then remembered that he had to work on the model of the resort development. Construction had already started, and a crew was at the proposed site removing trees and underbrush so they could move their equipment up the mountain. His father had said few trees would be lost and new ones would be planted once the construction was complete. But Alex was afraid the mountain would look barren. He knew his father was trying to be fair about the development, but it was a topic best not brought up on such a fine morning.

"You guys have a good day, too," Alex said, trying to sound bright and cheerful. But considering his acting skills were next to zero, he just wasn't convincing. In this respect, he wished he were more like Wendy. She could flash a fake smile and cheery face and people believed her, though Alex knew her well enough to tell when she was pretending. He gathered up his trusty backpack and boots and went out the door.

"Take plenty of water with you!" Alex's mother called "And wear a hat to keep out the cold."

On the porch and safely out of earshot, Alex groaned. *My mom, super prepared. She should be the Boy Scout, not me.* Still, Alex knew she was, as usual, right. It was good to keep hydrated when hiking. Alex put on his boots, took some water from a cooler on the porch, put on his hat, and was on his way. For once he didn't have to race to Michael's, so he could enjoy the refreshing breeze and the mountain scenery.

Today, the warblers were flying around and making noise. Alex wondered what they were chatting about. If Wendy were here, she'd be convinced that the birds were making plans to escape when Mount St. Helens erupted. Alex smiled. No matter how hard he tried to ignore a possible eruption and push it to the back of his mind, it kept floating to the front. Between Wendy's letters full of dire news and Michael's legends, there was no way to avoid the topic. *Ah, well, grin and bear it,* he thought.

Alex concluded there was no way the mountain could erupt on such an ideal sunny day. The only clouds were white and fluffy. Approaching Michael's place, Alex heard voices. *What's going on?* Alex didn't remember the hiking club planning an event today. He was pretty sure it was supposed to be just the two of them, but when Alex reached Michael's, he saw the driveway was full of cars and there were about twenty people on Michael's porch. And none of them were dressed for hiking, as they were all bundled up in preparation for the weather. Other than Michael, the only person Alex recognized was Jake, who worked with his mom part-time, giving tours on the weekend. Jake nodded at Alex, but he seemed antsy and was wearing camouflage clothes. *Clearly trying to remain hidden,* Alex thought.

"Ah, Alex, welcome," Michael greeted him.

What are you up to? Alex wondered.

An older woman, whom Alex had seen in the library, handed him a paintbrush. "Time to get to work, dear."

Next to her were several signs that read, "Stop the Development NOW!" Alex put down the brush on an open paint can. Obviously, they were going to stage a protest. Alex was against the development, but he wasn't willing to march against his father, either.

"I'm going to hike. I'll see you later, Michael," Alex mumbled. Then he shifted his backpack and walked back to the path.

"Enjoy yourself, son!" Michael called out. "We'll see you later."

I doubt it, Alex thought. It was one thing to argue with his father, but to actually protest?

Still, as Alex continued his climb, he wondered whether the protesters were right about this after all. *How could he betray his friend Smoky?* Alex figured the protest would be peaceful and the marchers were just taking a stand. *Justifying their actions,* Alex's conscience argued. *People need jobs, too,* was the response on the flip side.

Continuing up the trail, Alex shrugged off thoughts about the development. He reached his favorite spot, crawled under the welcoming branches, and settled in to draw. Today, instead of images of Samurai soldiers standing guard, the fir trees seemed to become lost souls swaying in the wind. Using shading, Alex drew teardrops on their branches. Alex was drawing from his heart, not anything he was looking at. Once he finished his third sketch, the teardrops on the sad trees had turned into a flood. Alex made a decision. He'd join the protest. He quickly packed his artist tools and raced back to Michael's lodge. Sweat was dripping down his back by the time he reached Michael's, but the driveway was empty. *They must be at the site.*

And as Alex marched toward the site, his steps grew stronger and stronger.

Alex no longer wavered in his feelings. He had to protect Spirit Lake and Smoky, even if that meant joining a demonstration against his father's company. They didn't necessarily need to stop the development, but maybe just scale it back. His father was reasonable, and Alex knew that in his heart his father loved the area as much as Alex and his mother did, so he was sure some sort of compromise could be reached. *At least, I hope so,* he thought.

When Alex reached the site, he saw that there were about fifteen people gathered. Apparently, some of those who had met at Michael's had changed their minds and returned home. *Not much of a protest,* Alex thought. Most of the protesters were closer to Michael's age, in their sixties and older, clearly making Alex the youngest one there. Alex didn't really know them, but he had seen most of them around town and he recognized a couple who were members of the hiking club. Alex didn't spot Jake. He must have concluded that being part of a protest might hurt him in finding or keeping a job next summer in a small town like Nighthawk. Jake admired Alex's parents, and Alex sensed that Jake's support of the protesters had lost out to the realization that his boss— Alex's mother—was married to the target of the protest, his father. *A no-win situation. Sort of like my position.* Alex recognized members of the local Audubon conservation society and nodded to them. Still, his conscience bothered him. His resolve was weakening. *What am I doing here? They don't need me.* Unlike Wendy, who was impulsive and acted first and thought about it later, Alex thought about his actions and was aware of their consequences. His mother said he was mature for his age, but Wendy said he was just a stick in the mud.

Alex started to retreat and then changed his mind. Memories of glorious times on Spirit Lake and the quiet and solitude his friend Smoky offered swept over him. Snapshots of those memories drifted through his mind. Alex remembered fishing on the lake in the early morning with his father and grandfather. At night, his grandfather had told Alex stories about how the lake was a sacred place to the local Native American tribes. Some of the stories were about the eruptions on Smoky, like Michael's, but his grandfather was such a good storyteller that Alex had been caught up in the stories and not by the fact that they were about volcanoes. Besides, he was younger and the stories had been more like vivid pictures than real events. Alex looked up at the clear, azure sky. The warm sun seemed to paint the lake and mountain in a golden glow. This was his vision of Smoky. *It shouldn't change.*

The postcard-perfect image made Alex turn back. If the development were built, the lake would be filled with motorboats, and the tranquility and peace that was Spirit Lake would be lost.

Once Alex reached the protesters, he gritted his teeth and picked up a sign that read, "Keep the Spirit of the Lake." Michael waved to him and Alex signaled back, hoisted the sign, and joined the group. There were already enough camps on the lake. His friend—good old Smoky—had to be protected. *Sorry, Dad,* he thought.

The group planned to march to the shores of Spirit Lake, where the crystal-clear blue water shone like a flawless sapphire. *Couldn't his father see the natural wonder of it all?* Alex had tried to convince his father that the project should be stopped, but his father, usually open-minded, said his company needed the work and it would create local jobs, all of which was good for the community. His father said it was carefully planned, including reforestation. The beauty of the lake and mountain would be enhanced, not lost. Alex didn't believe that.

"You're damaging my friend," Alex had cried, but his father had dismissed his feelings and told him he was overreacting. Typical teenager—and just barely a teen—his father had implied.

Alex's mother had broken her silence and declared the project off-limits for discussion.

"I'm not having our home turned into a verbal war zone," she proclaimed one night after they began raising their voices in making their points. So to keep the peace, the two had stopped debating about the project. The thought of construction tearing up the hundred-year-old trees, as well as new roads and houses popping up all around the wilderness lake, troubled Alex. His fist tightened on the sign. *How could anyone want to interfere with something as beautiful and tranquil as Spirit Lake?* He had no choice but to join the protests. It was the right thing to do. Still, Alex knew his father had good intentions. But what had Michael said? *Good intentions can't buy you a place in heaven.* Alex wasn't quite sure what that saying meant, but it sounded right.

Alex's father would be furious upon learning that Alex had joined the protesters. Considering the small size of the Spirit Lake community, his father would be certain to find out. *I'll deal with it when I get home*, Alex thought. Besides, since they couldn't talk about the project, maybe it wouldn't even come up. *Yeah, right. I never have that kind of luck.*

All around him, the protesters were chanting, "No changes to Spirit Lake!" Alex joined in, too. The group moved in rhythm to the chants. Step, chant, step, chant.

Alex appreciated that Spirit Lake was accessible almost all year-round. *This is the way the lake was meant to be. No engines roaring and boats speeding around.* Alex was even unhappy that the protesters were chanting so loudly, disturbing the quiet that Alex loved so much.

Alex scanned the area. There was no sign of his father, though some of the construction workers from his company were on the scene. Alex tried to blend into the group, hoping no one would spot him. *If only I had camouflage clothing.*

Alex wondered if the fishermen in the two canoes on the lake would join them; although probably sympathetic, they remained far from shore content to fish. *Sheep, Michael would have called them.* Alex stared at the lake, getting lost in it. Like a mantra, the same thoughts kept running through Alex's mind, as if they were on a continual loop. *Building expensive homes would disrupt the beauty and tranquility of the lake. The trees would be gone, and so would the animals that live on the mountain. Plus, those who bought summer homes wouldn't have the same respect and love for the area. They wouldn't appreciate "Smoking Mountain" and the lake.* Alex chanted louder. The development had to be stopped, or at least delayed. Alex saw Michael chanting and pumping his fist and nodded to him. Michael gave him a thumbs-up.

The police had quietly arrived and were watching the protesters for signs of potential violence. Alex hoped the demonstration would be peaceful, but several of the protesters were really upset. On the other side, the construction workers who were doing surveying work weren't pleased either. Soon those workers formed their own line of protests and started chanting, "Go home!" A few had even started their chainsaws, creating a deafening noise.

Alex knew the men needed the jobs, but sacrificing the lake was not the right solution. Alex wished his father's company could produce another plan. Soon the chanting turned into name-calling. *This is not good,* Alex thought. One wrong remark, and what was now just a shouting match could turn into a dangerous brawl.

Suddenly a protester slipped to the ground. *Did the earth just move?* Alex wondered. He could swear the ground had shifted, causing the protester to fall. He could almost hear Wendy saying, "That was a tremor. I'm right about your Smoky." No one else seemed to notice, so maybe it was just his imagination. Alex was glad Wendy wasn't there. She would have been positive the ground had shifted and was a sign that the mountain was about to erupt, proving her right. *No, Wendy.* The only eruption that Alex was positive was about to happen was the clash between the protesters and the construction workers.

Alex moved to assist the woman but felt a hand on his back, and before he could react, he was lying face down on the ground. Someone stepped on his hand, and Alex cried out. Another man helped Alex to his feet. Soon the police were breaking up the two groups. Alex was ordered to leave the area. At first Alex resisted, then he spotted his father racing down to talk to the police. He was there to protect his workers. *You're on the wrong side, Dad.*

Still, Alex wasted no time in retreating and disappearing into the dispersing crowd. He glanced over his shoulder and saw his father talking with the police. Alex hoped his father hadn't seen him. But he'd worry about that later. More pressing was discarding his sign. NOW. Michael approached Alex and took it from him.

"You'd best be gone, son," Michael advised. He didn't have to tell Alex twice. Alex scurried home.

CHAPTER 8

Wendy shifted her backpack on her shoulders. Once again, it was overloaded from the books on Mount Vesuvius and Pompeii crammed into it. *I should have left one of them at home,* she thought. *Alex is NOT going to read them, and I have them practically memorized.* Wendy sighed. Suddenly she realized that her mother was speaking to her.

She cautioned Wendy. "You know the rules. Don't talk to strangers. Stay on the bus and don't get off until the Nighthawk/Mount St. Helens stop. Alex and his parents will pick you up there. Have you got your ticket?"

Wendy's mother trusted her, but it still made her nervous sending Wendy off alone on the bus. She knew it was safe, and Wendy had made the trip for almost a year, but she still worried. "Once you reach Alex's house, make sure you call me…"

"I'll be waiting by the phone," Wendy finished her mother's statement.

The two hugged and laughed.

"Don't be such a smarty pants," her mother said.

"Love you, Mom" Wendy said as she moved to the line of passengers boarding the bus. Her mother smiled and waved. If Wendy didn't know better, she could swear her mother had tears in her eyes. *I'm only going an hour or so away and I'll be at your best friend's home. Mothers,* Wendy thought. Wendy climbed on the bus and took a window seat. She waved one last time at her mother as the bus drove away. The bus left behind clouds of smoke. *Like a mini-volcano,* Wendy mused.

Wendy pulled out her book, unwound her scarf, and began reading about Mount Vesuvius.

Lost in her reading, she almost missed the bus driver announce the Nighthawk/Mount St. Helens stop. Wendy shoved the book into her backpack and leaped out of her seat.

"Take it easy, miss, and please sit down until the bus comes to a full stop," the bus driver ordered.

Wendy fell back into her seat. Looking out the window, she spotted Alex. She wondered why his jacket was open. Smiling, she noticed that he was wearing the T-shirt she had sent him. It had an exploding mountain on it, and under the image was the line, "I erupt for art!" Wendy was pleased Alex was wearing it. She had designed and printed the shirt especially for him. It was much cooler than the ghost one she had given him last year. Ghosts and Alex didn't really go together, though she had liked the tagline: "Watch me disappear." Alex was too practical and levelheaded to believe in spirits. Still, he had been a good sport when Wendy kept dragging him to the supposedly haunted lodge at all hours. However, Alex yelling "BOO!" at her continually had become tiresome.

Alex had told Wendy that that was how he felt with her howling, so she had given up that greeting—well, most of the time. The occasional howl was good for him; it kept him on his paws. Wendy chuckled at her own joke.

The bus pulled into its stop, and Wendy charged down the aisle. The bus driver shook his head and opened the door, letting Wendy race out. She jumped into Alex's mother's waiting arms and then punched Alex. "Hey, Van Gogh, good to see you. I've got books for you to read."

Alex smiled. *Of course, you do.* Still, he was glad his friend was there. Wendy noticed that Alex and his father were kind of distant with each other, but she didn't say anything.

The four of them climbed into the station wagon as Alex proclaimed, "Home, there's no place like home."

And your beloved Smoky, Wendy thought.

Once in the car, Wendy couldn't contain herself. "So have there been any quakes, Aunt Jenny?"

Alex's mother chuckled. Wendy was not wasting any time and, as usual, had a one-track mind. "No, dear. All is quiet on the volcano front."

Wendy nodded. Alex could tell she was disappointed.

"Mom, tell Wendy what the geologists said about Mount St. Helens," Alex suggested. He knew that the news would interest Wendy.

"Well, they have concluded that Mount St. Helens is active," Mrs. Porter said. Wendy couldn't help herself and smiled at the news. Alex mouthed the word "active" with air quotes.

Ignoring him, Mrs. Porter continued. "So we are all on alert and should stay in contact at all times. Until further notice, camping overnight is out. In fact, I want you kids to make sure you take the walkie-talkie along on your hikes." Both Alex and Wendy were familiar with the hand-held radio device used to send and receive voice messages over a small area.

"Of course we will," Wendy agreed.

Alex almost laughed out loud. He knew Wendy would do anything his mother said as long as they got to hike the mountain and check out what was happening. Alex could imagine the wheels in Wendy's head turning.

"I'm sure it won't erupt this weekend," Wendy said. *But you wish it would,* Alex thought. Wendy told Mrs. Porter about what her mother was doing, even though Wendy was sure the two had talked recently to confirm the details of her trip. Wendy was struck by how different the two women were in terms of personality, yet they were best friends. *Sort of like Alex and me,* Wendy thought.

Since Wendy's arrival, Alex and his father had not spoken to each other. Wendy was not totally surprised; she had overheard her mother saying that she was sure Alex and his father would work things out. Wendy had assumed it probably had to do with Alex's father's resort development. Alex had hinted in a letter that he was opposed to it, but Wendy also knew better than to get in the middle of a family feud.

Besides, her focus was on Mount St. Helens. And an eruption would certainly stop any new construction in the area. Wendy turned to Alex.

"So, Alex, you can read the book on Mount Vesuvius tonight and then we can discuss it while we hike tomorrow. There are some signs we can look for, and maybe we can figure out what will happen and predict when *it* might happen." Wendy used the word *it* as if it were some sort of secret code. *NOT*, Alex thought.

"Um, okay," Alex replied. *As if I have a choice.* Somehow Alex knew he wouldn't do much sketching this weekend, but by the time they reached the house, he was caught up in Wendy's world of volcanoes, and his head was spinning. She had gone on about the different types of volcanoes, how they formed, and what made them erupt.

They entered the house, and Wendy dropped off her backpack in the guest room. Alex followed her. "Relax and take a load off," Alex teased her.

"I will," Wendy shot back. She pulled out the book on Mount Vesuvius and tossed it to Alex. Alex caught it, pretending the weight of the book had knocked him down.

"Funny move, Alex," Wendy said as she pursed her lips but then laughed. "It's full of useful but fun information. You'll enjoy it."

Alex just nodded and took the book to his room. He tossed it on his bed. A little "light" reading. *Should help me fall asleep,* Alex thought. He was eager to get hiking.

"Come on, Wendy!" Alex called. "We can go down to the lake before supper." Soon Wendy joined him, and the two were out the door. "Be back in an hour. And take water," his mother said as the two left for Spirit Lake.

"Race you!" Wendy yelled, and she took off. Alex watched Wendy sprint, totally surprised by her movements. *Wow, she really can run. Who knew?* Alex caught up with her, and the two settled down into a brisk walk. "You walk as fast as Michael," Alex commented as the two reached the shores of Spirit Lake.

"I take it that's a compliment," Wendy said with a laugh. "How is he?"

"He's well. He's organizing protests against the development," Alex stated, waiting for Wendy's reaction.

Wendy picked up a smooth stone and skimmed it across the lake. It bounced four times before disappearing. "Well, the lake is impressive as always. So, I can understand why Michael doesn't want things to change, but time does march on."

"I suppose," Alex muttered as he skimmed a rock. He wondered if Wendy was on her father's side. "Still, it seems like a mistake."

"I'm sure your dad will be careful. You know he loves the area about as much as you do." Wendy wanted to discuss volcanoes, but she knew her friend had to get his feelings off his chest first. *Why did boys have to overthink things?* Wendy wondered. Alex was more guilty of this than most.

"You're right," Alex smiled. "And I hate to be the bearer of bad news, but I don't think you'll see any eruptions this weekend."

Wendy ignored her friend's bait. She wasn't about to debate when Mount St. Helens would erupt, since no one knew for sure. "No, I'm wishing for some minor earthquake activity this weekend."

When Wendy finished speaking, Alex could have sworn the ground trembled, but because Wendy didn't react, Alex assumed it must have been his imagination.

Then he noticed how quiet it was. Not a creature was active, apart from human ones— not in the sky, not in the water, and not on the mountain. Alex almost told Wendy what Michael had said about the birds and animals and their odd behavior, but he decided against it. Besides, Wendy was probably thinking about Mount Vesuvius. It was better if she was focused on an ancient volcanic eruption rather than Smoky. The two returned to the house in silence. As they wiped their feet on the porch rug, Alex looked out at the lake one last time. You could hear tiny ripples of water lapping on the shore and nothing else. Tomorrow they'd explore Smoky and visit Michael. Alex wondered if Michael's joints were still twitching. His trembling, which Michael kept saying meant Smoky was getting ready to blow, would be one more "fact" for Wendy to conclude Mount St. Helens was poised to erupt. And of course, Michael would agree with her. Alex sighed. He was outnumbered and there was no point in arguing with either friend.

CHAPTER 9

Wendy opened her eyes and for a moment wondered where she was. Quickly, it became clear. She was at Alex's house, of course. Wendy got out of bed and went to the door, listening to the voices coming from the kitchen. Mr. Porter was saying that he wanted to show Wendy the model of the development, with Alex countering that he was sure Wendy wasn't interested. So, the two were still at odds over the development. *Thanks for putting words in my mouth, Alex,* Wendy thought. *Now I'm in the middle! Ugh, sometimes Alex just didn't know when to keep his mouth shut.* Wendy could hear her mother's voice in her head: "Pot calling the kettle black."

Wendy groaned, got dressed quickly, and plastered a smile on her face. She hoped she could think of a way to avoid discussing the development, otherwise the day would be ruined before it began.

"Morning, all," Wendy chirped, hoping she could divert everyone's attention. "Well, no earthquake last night, huh?" Wendy's laugh sounded forced. Alex's mom looked over and smiled. Wendy was sure she was on her side.

"Have some breakfast, Wendy, and then the two of you can be off. I've got several groups to take on tours, so we might pass each other on the trails. Unless, of course, Alex takes you on his secret path." Alex's mother made a gesture of air quotes with her hands when she said "secret path."

"Mom," Alex started to complain but then just laughed. Once again, his mother knew exactly what was going to happen. *Maybe she does have ESP or something,* Alex thought. *Nah, that would be silly.*

"Well, whatever you do, I've left you ham and cheese sandwiches—mustard on yours, Wendy—and there's water in the cooler. Remember…"

"You need to stay hydrated when you're hiking." Alex and Wendy finished the sentence. All four laughed. *No development discussion. Hurray*, Wendy thought.

Alex packed the sandwiches and told Wendy to get her backpack and he'd wait for her on the porch. "Leave the books in your room, Wendy!" Alex yelled from the porch. *I hope she heard me. Last thing we need is a backpack that weighs a ton.* Soon Wendy joined him, and the two started off.

"You want to explore first or visit Michael?" Alex asked.

"Whatever you want to do," Wendy replied. She looked away and smiled. She knew Alex wanted her to decide, so it would be fun to make him choose.

"No, really, which do you want to do?" Alex asked, trying to be patient.

"Whatever you want to do is fine with me," Wendy replied.

"No, really, which do you want to do?" Alex tried to keep the irritation out of his voice. *Make a decision.* They were at a fork in the trails, and if they went left they'd be on their way to Michael's, and if they went right they'd be on one of the trails to the summit.

"No, really, *whatever* you want to do is fine with me," Wendy said, pretending to cough to hide her laughter.

"Fine, we'll hike to the summit," Alex replied tersely, and he set off on the trail. Wendy stood at the fork. Alex whipped around. "What?" he said, clearly irritated.

"I thought we'd go to Michael's," Wendy said with a straight face. Alex stomped down the trail to the fork.

"FINE," he muttered. As he started up the trail to Michael's, he heard Wendy's laugh and turned around.

"Gotcha!" she cried. "Come on, let's hike to the summit and stop at Michael's on the way back down."

Alex shook his head and then chuckled. She'd "gotten" him. The two hiked up the trail, enjoying the peace and quiet. Luckily, there were no other hikers on the trail yet, so they had it to themselves. Both took off their hats and unzipped their jackets, as they developed a sweat even though it was only March.

"This is nice," Wendy observed. She pulled out her camera and started taking pictures.

"Do you want to stop so you can get some better shots?" Alex asked.

"No, these are just for my log," Wendy said.

"Your log?" Alex wasn't sure why Wendy wanted photos for a log.

"Yes, these will be the 'before' pictures," she said. "Then I'll take photos after the eruption, and we'll be able to compare them. It will be a visual record."

"Gee, Wendy, that sounds a little morbid," Alex commented. "Besides, you can't be sure there will be an eruption."

"Oh, there will be, trust me," Wendy said with complete confidence. "And scientists need to keep a record of their work."

Alex decided it was best not to say anything and just kept hiking. Once they were halfway up the trail, the two stopped and had their sandwiches. It wasn't quite lunch time, but the two were hungry. Alex pulled out the food and the canteen. He looked forward to sipping the cool water. Alex was half-tempted to switch the sandwiches and give Wendy the one with mayonnaise, as he knew she hated "sticky" bread. The idea of getting back at her for her teasing earlier appealed to him. In all the years that Alex had known Wendy, she'd only eat mustard on her sandwiches. When she was younger, somehow bread with mayonnaise had stuck to the roof of her mouth. Since then, she had avoided eating all "sticky" bread. Alex handed Wendy her sandwich, and she immediately checked to make sure it was the mustard one.

"Hey, I wouldn't give you the wrong sandwich," Alex said, sounding wounded.

"Right, like you never have before?" Wendy replied. "You know the old saying: Trick me once, my fault; trick me twice, no dice."

"I don't think that's really the saying," Alex laughed.

"You get the point." Wendy replied through a mouthful of sandwich. "Hey, share the water."

Alex passed her the canteen. The two finished their sandwiches and enjoyed the silence.

"I love how quiet it is here," Wendy observed.

"You might ask Michael about the silence," Alex said.

"Why?" Wendy asked.

"Oh, he'll explain it." Alex wanted to see if Wendy fell for the "silence of the birds" as a clue that Mount St. Helens was about to erupt—though Alex had to admit, in the book Wendy had given him, there were references to the animals going silent as they tried to escape Mount Vesuvius before the eruption. Maybe Michael's theory wasn't that far off. Of course, Alex would deny it might be true.

The two finally reached the top of the trail. Wendy immediately began taking pictures of the summit. "It looks like a perfect cone, doesn't it?" Wendy said as she snapped away. "You think it's really old, but actually Mount St. Helens is a young volcano in geological terms."

Wendy paused to make sure Alex was paying attention and then continued, "It took about 2,200 years to make that perfect shape. Of course, if it erupts, the whole shape of the mountain will change."

From happiness to sadness in zero to twenty seconds—way to go, Wendy, Alex thought.

"Let's head down to Michael's?" Alex hoisted his backpack and started down the trail, assuming

Wendy would follow. Alex felt the ground shake, heard a scream, and whipped around. Wendy was on the ground and her camera was laying on the path. Alex raced over to her.

"Are you okay?" he asked. "Anything broken?" If that were true, Alex wasn't sure he could carry her down the mountain.

"I'm okay." Wendy stood and brushed herself off. "Where's my camera?"

Alex picked it up and handed it to her.

"Luckily, it seems to be OK," she said. "I wish I had a tape recorder. It would have been great to get the sounds of the earthquake."

"I don't think that was an earthquake, Wendy. It was more like a mild tremor, and besides, what would you record?" Alex was trying to downplay the event, but Wendy wasn't buying it.

"No, that was more than a tremor, Alex," she retorted. "Face it. Your mountain is going to blow soon."

Alex would have been more upset if his friend weren't so excited.

"Fine, maybe that was a *minor* quake, but it's stopped and no eruption followed," Alex said.

Wendy said, "Oh, Alex, it's the first sign—you know, the first stage. Trust me, there will be more quakes, and no matter how gentle or small they seem, it is not good news. It means things are building up inside Mount St. Helens. Come on—let's get to Michael's. I want to hear what he has to say."

Wendy raced off, and Alex had no choice but to follow.

I'm not sure I want to hear what Michael has to say, Alex thought. With her flaming red hair shining in the sun, she looked like what Alex imagined lava looked like: a ball of fire racing down the mountain. He hoped they would never witness that horrifying sight for real.

Michael was on his porch sweeping up a plant that had just fallen over. "Hey, Van Gogh and Miss Wendy," Michael said in a calm voice. Alex was pleased to see he didn't look upset or ruffled.

"Did you two feel the quake?" Michael asked.

Wendy turned to give Alex an "I told you so" look and then replied, "Yes, we sure did. It knocked me over, but we're fine. It's the first stage isn't it? Mount St. Helens is going to erupt."

You don't have to sound quite so thrilled, Alex thought.

"I think it is, I think it is."

Michael motioned the two up on the porch. "Notice no birds singing. That's another sign."

Wendy nodded her head in total agreement. *The oracles of Mount St. Helens are off,* she thought.

"How long do you think before Mount St. Helens actually erupts?" Wendy asked eagerly.

"Well, I think you have time for a glass of lemonade first. You look a little parched,"

Michael replied wryly. He went inside and returned with three cold glasses of lemonade. "Here, have this. It's refreshing, even in the winter."

The three sipped their drinks each wondering if there was going to be another quake, but everything remained still except for Wendy, who kept leaping from one foot to the other in anticipation. "I think you can relax, Wendy. If another quake were going to hit, it would have happened by now," Michael said.

Disappointed, Wendy sat on the stairs.

Michael continued. "However, as I told Alex, my bones have really been aching, so I do think this is just the beginning, but there's no telling when 'my girl' might blow."

"Your bones predict the weather?" Wendy asked.

Alex groaned. *Seriously? Talk about two peas in a pod,* he thought.

"Well, I like to think I can read them, but some people don't believe me." Michael stared at Alex who looked away.

"That's because someone doesn't want to believe their precious mountain is an ACTIVE volcano, but we know it is, don't we, Michael?" Wendy stared at Alex.

"Fine, maybe you both are right," Alex said. "But don't forget, the mountain hasn't had an eruption in over a hundred years, so one little quake doesn't mean Smoky is going to blow her stack."

Alex gulped down his lemonade.

"No, it doesn't mean she will, but all the signs do point to an eruption happening," Michael said. "It's really just a matter of when." Wendy nodded her head furiously.

Alex answered, "Well, if that's true, maybe you should come down to our house, so then we'd be able to evacuate safely." He was worried his stubborn friend would refuse to evacuate.

"That's not a bad idea," Wendy said. She wanted Michael to be safe, and Alex's family lived close enough to the main road that they could easily escape if anything happened. Michael's lodge was too far up the mountain.

"I thank you for the offer, but I'm not leaving 'my girl.'" Michael smiled at his two friends. "At least, not yet. However, you two had better mosey on home, as I'm sure your folks are worried, Alex."

"Alright, but remember, you promised you'll leave if any more quakes hit," Alex said. Michael didn't answer but just shooed the two off on their way.

"I hope he will evacuate," Alex said softly.

"Me, too," Wendy replied.

For once she was silent. When the two reached the house, Alex's parents came out to the porch and welcomed them both.

"Glad you're here safe and sound, though I wasn't worried," Alex's mother said as she squeezed the two of them in a bear hug.

Right, Mom, Alex thought.

CHAPTER 10

Wendy woke up to the phone ringing; she was sure it was her mother checking up on her. The news last night had reported the tremor and announced how the geologists were tracking what was happening at Mount St. Helens. Wendy had been glued to the news, but Alex had quickly changed the channel to *WKRP in Cincinnati*, a comedy series set in a rock music radio station. Wendy would have preferred to watch singer Barbara Mandrel and her show, but she knew Alex hated country music, so she didn't complain and actually found the show funny. Listening to Alex's mother's conversation, Wendy pictured Mount St. Helens blasting away.

Alex's mother told Wendy's mother that even though they had experienced a small tremor, no further earthquakes had happened and Wendy was totally safe. Wendy feared that her mother would demand she take an earlier bus home, but Aunt Jenny obviously had convinced her mother that all was fine. Letting out a sigh of relief, Wendy threw on her clothes and went downstairs. Alex and his family were eating breakfast.

"Hey, Miss Sleepy Head, want to see the models?" Alex's father asked. Wendy avoided looking at Alex, as she was sure he was rolling his eyes.

"Sure, let me grab some juice." Alex's mom handed Wendy a glass full. She and Alex's father walked into his home office. Alex could hear his father explaining the development and Wendy exclaiming how great it was.

Before Alex could object, his mother held up her hand. "Not now, Alex. Your father is under a lot of pressure, and these quakes don't help."

Alex nodded. As usual, his mother was right.

"Do you really think Mount St. Helens is going to erupt soon?" Alex asked.

"Don't tell Wendy, but I do. Every time I talk with David and the other geologists, it seems like it is just a matter of *when*, not *if*. I don't want to worry Susan because I know Wendy will have a tantrum if her mother doesn't let her return here. You have to promise me that the two of you will be careful, stay together, and keep the walkie-talkie with you at all times."

"I promise," Alex said solemnly.

"You promise what?" Wendy asked.

"Oh, to make sure we're back in time for you to catch your bus," Alex replied.

"We will, Aunt Jenny, don't worry." Wendy said with a smile. Alex's mother nodded.

"Alex, I had an idea," Wendy said.

Alex groaned. He had images of the two of them descending into the volcano. *We're not in* Journey to the Center of the Earth,

Alex thought. *This is not a Jules Verne novel.* "What's your idea?"

"Let's make Michael a volcano emergency kit!" Wendy exclaimed. She was so excited and proclaimed her idea so loudly that Alex was certain Michael had probably heard her all the way up the mountain.

"I think that's a marvelous idea, Wendy," Alex's mother declared.

"So do I," echoed his father. *Of course you do; she claimed she loved your development.*

Alex sighed. He knew what he would be doing this morning. "Well then, let's get started. What's in an emergency volcano kit anyway?"

"Oh, trust me, I've researched it. I know." Wendy boasted and then ran up to retrieve items from her backpack.

Alex's mother laughed. "It will be fun, Alex. Relax!"

Alex nodded. *I have no choice.* However, he knew it really would be fun.

"Here, I have a list. We need masks..." Alex started to ask if they were Halloween masks.

Wendy cut him off. "Don't even start, Alex. You know I don't mean Halloween masks. We need the kind that painters use to keep out the dust. We also need eye goggles and plenty of water and snacks that don't have to be heated or cooled."

"How about going to the hardware store with me?" Alex's father suggested. "I'm sure you can get the masks and goggles there. We can get the snacks in the supermarket."

"I'll bake some crispy rice treats," his mother chimed in. "You can give some to Michael, and Wendy, you can take some back on the bus with you. They will stay for a long time and don't need to be refrigerated—plus, they are nourishing."

She looked at her husband and the kids. "Well, they're kind of healthy."

Alex's father nodded, and Alex and Wendy laughed.

Alex, his father, and Wendy set off on a short drive to the hardware store. Once they arrived, Wendy took out her list, and they were racing around the store trying to find what they needed. Alex's father had said he'd go buy the snacks and then return to pay for the items. Wendy had offered to pay, but Alex's father had told her to save her money.

As they waited at the checkout counter, the clerk asked if they were planning some painting or blasting. Wendy, in her most serious tone, said that they were making a volcano emergency kit. The clerk looked confused.

"Mount St. Helens is going to erupt any day now," Wendy declared triumphantly. Alex wanted to crawl under the counter.

"You don't say," the clerk drawled. Wendy was about to explain why Mount St. Helens would erupt, but Alex put his hand on her arm, and luckily she remained silent. Alex's father entered the store and paid for their purchases.

"Preparing for a volcano, huh, Tom?" the clerk grinned. Like many who lived there, the clerk knew little about the history of Mount St. Helens and the fact that it was an active volcano. Even though the recent tremors and quakes had been felt in Nighthawk and neighboring towns, few took it as a sign that Mount St. Helens was ready to blow. Alex's father just nodded and shrugged, as if to say, "Kids, what can I say?" Wendy took her purchases and huffed on her way to the car.

"Wendy, calm down," Alex pleaded. He didn't want their day ruined. "The clerk isn't an expert on volcanoes like you are."

Wendy nodded, somewhat appeased. Alex's father gave him an approving nod. Still, on the way home, there was very little conversation.

"How was your shopping trip?" Alex's mother asked when the three entered the house. Wendy remained silent, while Alex told his mom that everything was fine and they had bought everything they needed.

Alex's father whispered, "The clerk didn't believe Wendy about the danger of an eruption, so she's not in the best mood."

"It's true. Too many people don't seriously believe that Mount St. Helens will erupt soon," Alex's mother said. "And you can't blame them. After all, the mountain has been silent for over a hundred years and has become a tourist destination. A lot of the people I guide don't know the difference between a dormant volcano and an active one. Most people think the only volcanoes that would erupt in the U.S. are in Hawaii, where the ring of fire is located."

"Well, Michael believes the mountain will erupt, so I'm sure he will appreciate the emergency kit," Alex's father said. "Maybe it will make him realize he should evacuate." Alex's father hoped that what he said would prove true. If Michael remained stubborn and refused to leave "his girl," the chances of rescuing him would be slim.

Alex came down to the kitchen and announced, "We're done with the kit. We've packed masks so Michael can breathe in clouds of ash, goggles to protect his eyes from the heat and hot ash flakes, and snacks and water for him to consume when he loses power. He'd be safe until he is rescued. Of course, it would be easier if he just came and stayed with us, but you know how stubborn he is."

Alex's mom added, "I'm sure he'll realize he has to leave. As much as he loves the mountain, he's a practical man, and common sense will rule the day."

She began boxing up the crispy rice treats. "Here, add these to the kit. There's enough for you to share with him when you reach his house."

"Thanks, Mom." Alex looked at his father. "And thanks, Dad, for paying for the supplies and supporting Wendy."

"Hey, we're in this together," his father said. "Go 'Team Mount St. Helens!'" Alex and his father high-fived. Alex's mother was happy the two seemed to put their disagreement behind them. Wendy walked in with Michael's kit and joined the celebration.

"Come on, Van Gogh, let's deliver our super-duper emergency kit," Wendy commanded. Her camera hung around her neck. Alex grabbed a walkie-talkie, and the two set off for Michael's.

Alex's parents watched the two from the porch. "You know, we probably should buy some masks and goggles for ourselves," Alex's mother said.

"Already ahead of you," Alex's father replied as he pulled out three masks and goggles. The two laughed and tried them on.

"We look like aliens," Alex's father said.

"Yes, but you know my motto: always be prepared," Alex's mother said.

CHAPTER 11

Alex hit the "send" button on the walkie-talkie. "We're here. Over and out." Alex waited for the reply.

"Message received," Alex's mother said loud and clear.

"It's like a World War II spy movie," Wendy commented.

"All of this reminds me of wartime London and the blitzes," Michael said, pointing to the walkie-talkie and the emergency kit. Michael clearly had a World War II story to share, but Alex and Wendy distracted him by handing him the emergency kit.

"What's in this?" Michael asked.

Wendy answered, "Things you'll need in a volcanic emergency. You have masks so you can breathe easier, goggles to protect your eyes, and food and water. This will tide you over until you leave or are rescued." She paused and then continued, "Though you should go stay with Alex and his family right now."

"Yeah, Michael, you should come to our house. We have a spare bedroom and we'd love to have you," Alex pleaded.

"Appreciate the offer, Van Gogh, but you know how I feel about 'my girl.' She's stood by me all these years, so I should do the same for her." Michael peeked into the kit. "Hey, I see your mom made my favorite treats. Let's have some now."

The three finished their snacks in silence. But, a chorus of melodious song sparrows serenaded them, so Alex was satisfied that Smoky would remain fast asleep at least for now. Still, all the precautions and talk about the eruption were making Alex anxious. *Would they be able to rescue Michael once Mount St. Helens erupted?* he wondered. Wendy guessed they'd have a window of about an hour to escape, depending on the size of the eruption. And from what Alex had learned about Mount Vesuvius, that much time to escape seemed unlikely. Well, there was no use worrying about it now; Michael clearly wasn't moving. Besides, they did have an alternate plan.

"Hey, Wendy, should we hike up the mountain? You can take some pictures for your log," Alex said. Wendy immediately perked up. "That was the plan, Vincent." Alex knew Wendy was in a better mood since she was changing his nickname. He preferred "Vincent" over "Van Gogh," though he knew Wendy was just showing off her knowledge that Van Gogh's first name was Vincent. Still, it made Alex smile. And her urge to howl at him had finally and totally disappeared, which was even better.

The two helped Michael clean the kitchen and then started up the path. They heard Michael call out, "Hey, Vincent Van Gogh, you might need this." Michael held up the walkie-talkie. Embarrassed, Alex quickly made a U-turn and took the walkie-talkie.

"Better safe than sorry," Michael said. Alex nodded and hitched the device to his belt.

While waiting, Wendy snapped some photos of Michael and his lodge. "I'm sure Michael would want photos of his home whether anything happens or not." Wendy said. Alex agreed as the two walked on silently.

As they neared the summit, Wendy began snapping more photos. Neither had the urge to talk; instead, they simply enjoyed the view and its splendor. As they headed down the trail, both wondered if Smoky and all they loved about the mountain would soon be just a memory. Alex hit "send" on the walkie-talkie, informing his parents that they were on their way home. Looking around the trail at a landscape that might soon disappear, Alex had an almost pained expression on his face.

"You know that nature adapts and the plants and wildlife will all come back after the eruption," Wendy said, hoping to comfort her friend. Alex nodded, but even if true, it was cold comfort. Alex was glad he had all his paintings of Smoky and Spirit Lake. He'd preserve those images forever.

When the pair returned to Alex's house, his parents suggested they stop at their favorite diner before Wendy caught the bus back to Portland. Alex readily agreed. The treats had been delicious, but he was ready for a real meal. Wendy packed her belongings. She left Alex a note as a surprise. Her message was that Smoky would rebuild herself, different, but more beautiful than ever.

Soon, it was time for Wendy to leave for home. "Thanks for the meal and the weekend. I had a great time," Wendy said as she climbed out of the car. She pulled out her ticket and turned to Alex and his parents. She punched Alex. "Finish your paintings, Van Gogh. I want to see them when I'm here next."

"What? You're coming back?" Alex grinned.

"Ha, you know I am," Wendy snapped back.

"Well, I'll warn Mount St. Helens not to erupt until you return," Alex promised. Wendy playfully punched him again and then hugged Alex's parents.

"Come back soon, Wendy," his parents said.

"I will. Keep me posted on EVERYTHING!" Wendy exclaimed.

Alex knew Wendy would call as often as her mother would permit. *I probably should keep a journal like Thoreau,* Alex thought. *I can then share my observations with Wendy.*

Wendy boarded the bus and grabbed a window seat. She gazed at Alex, who pretended the Earth was shaking, and did a silly dance. Wendy shook her head and then gave him a thumbs-up. Little did the two know that Alex's reaction would soon become a reality. Wendy settled into her seat and decided to dream about Mount St. Helens as she existed now. For once, Wendy had no desire to read about volcanoes, as it was all becoming too real.

CHAPTER 12

March 1980 became a month of earthquakes. Alex's mother announced that a new system of seismographs at the University of Washington had gone into operation. This included carefully monitoring earthquake activity in the Cascade region. The focus was on Mount St. Helens, the youngest volcano in the mountain chain and the most likely to erupt. Stories began appearing in the news about how the mountain had been quiet for over a hundred years, but now geologists were warning that she had come alive in full force. As Michael had warned, "his girl" was getting ready to burst. No one could deny that the constant quakes and tremors were proof that Smoky was very active. All the local talk was about how and when residents would evacuate. Thus far, teams had been assembling evacuation plans, but no orders to leave the area had been issued.

As expected, as soon as Mount St. Helens became news in Portland, Wendy phoned Alex about every other night. Alex remained calm and explained that they had had a series of quakes, but so far just minor ones. Nothing had registered high on the Richter scale. Yes, Alex admitted Wendy had been right and Mount St. Helens had been active. Wendy kept peppering Alex with questions, many of which he couldn't answer.

Alex simply repeated that she hadn't missed anything. In fact, he had convinced his mother to tell Wendy the same thing, but Alex didn't tell Wendy that the quakes were becoming stronger. If Alex had shared that information, Wendy might try to hop the night bus to Nighthawk.

Clearly, Wendy was frustrated she wasn't there. Alex could tell from the tone of Wendy's voice that she desperately wanted to be "where the action was." Hearing Alex's reports did not make her feel better, plus he was overwhelmed by her endless questions. Luckily, both his parents followed the news and kept in constant touch with their geologist friends, so Alex had convinced his parents to compose a report to share with Wendy. So far the reports had kept her satisfied. Alex, however, knew that it was a short-term solution.

Because of the seismic activity around Mount St. Helens, the April school vacation schedule had been moved up. So, Alex had spent more time with Michael, but still failed to convince him to stay with his family. Alex was so frustrated that he even considered not visiting Michael for a time. He thought his friend was being foolish and that staying put would accomplish nothing. Alex's parents had no more luck than Alex in persuading him to leave, even just temporarily. Michael, as Wendy would say, was a "lost cause."

Wendy had even written Michael, filling her letter with facts on the dangers of him remaining on his property. Michael had shared the letter with Alex, and it had shocked him. Images of being buried under a river of lava or choking on ash were gruesome. Images from Wendy's books on Vesuvius kept surfacing in his mind. Alex would do about anything to prevent his friend from turning into a mummified figure. When the family realized that Michael was being unreasonable, Alex's mother talked with the geologists and the evacuation teams, and they put Michael at the top of their list to evacuate when Mount St. Helens did erupt. But it still didn't calm Alex.

On March 20th, a larger quake was recorded. It reached a magnitude of 4.2 on the Richter scale, and even though it was deep beneath Mount St. Helens, it started off a round-the-clock watch. The quake had triggered avalanches. Logging on the mountain had stopped since the logs floating in the rivers were deemed a hazard. Alex had visions of the area needing Paul Bunyan to come to their rescue. Would this ever end?

No one, not even the geologic experts, was sure when Mount St. Helens would erupt. Alex wished the ancient Chinese had invented a volcano machine instead of one that predicated earthquakes!

Alex's mother canceled all of her scheduled tours. More importantly, his father shelved plans for the resort development. With the threatening occurrences around Smoky, the idea of vacation homes now seemed far-fetched. Alex and his father became united in their worry about what would happen when Mount St. Helens erupted. Alex had joined the Wendy camp of thinking when it came to Smoky. Luckily, Wendy never said, "I told you so," though Alex was sure she thought so each time she called.

The evacuation team regularly visited Michael but had no luck in convincing him to leave. His lodge was just on the boundary of the danger zone, so he couldn't be forced to evacuate. Even witnessing his neighbors retreat to safer areas didn't faze him. Michael declared he saw no reason to leave "his girl."

How about if you stay, you'll die, Alex thought, but he refrained from voicing that fear because if he said it aloud, it might be like an omen and come true. At least Michael practiced putting on the mask and goggles, an encouraging sign that he took the possible eruption of Smoky seriously.

One night during a call with Wendy, the house began shaking uncontrollably, and the phone line went dead. A picture fell off the wall, shattering the glass frame. Huddled together in fear, Alex and his parents were trembling nearly as badly as the house. They sat in the dark, using flashlights and praying that the power would be restored in the morning. Fortunately, the weather was mild for that time of year. His father promised to drive to Nighthawk the next day and buy a generator.

"I hope they have at least one left," Alex mused. Uncertainty filled the shaken house, and no one slept easily that night.

Alex felt like his family was living in a war zone. Some weeks more than a hundred earthquakes, most of them minor, were recorded. Some roads had buckled, trees had fallen, and houses had shifted on their foundations. Wendy's mother had forbidden her from visiting Alex until the danger of the quakes passed. Wendy, of course, was frustrated from possibly missing out on the experience of a lifetime. Alex reassured Wendy that she was better off and safer in Portland. Alex jokingly asked if he could join her, but Wendy told him to stay put and record EVERY detail. Alex promised to do so, even though it was an empty promise. He had to follow his parents' orders. However, he did begin sketching what he thought Smoky would look like if she did erupt. Gone were the evergreen Samurai soldiers. Their gentle "teardrops" on the tree limbs had been replaced by streaking balls of fire. Now the evergreens were floating out of Smoky's cone. After a few days, Alex became discouraged and had to stop drawing.

Whenever a quake was felt, Alex was glad Wendy was safe, but Wendy, being *WENDY*, claimed Portland had experienced minor quakes, too. Alex wasn't sure how much she was exaggerating, but his mother said the earthquakes could be felt even miles away. His parents discussed leaving the Nighthawk area, even though they were supposedly in a safe zone and did not have to evacuate.

CHAPTER 13

In the following days, conditions around Nighthawk became calmer, at least temporarily. Alex had been rubbing his lava rock and praying for the quakes to stop. It seemed as if his wish might have been granted, but then on March 25th, another huge quake hit. The tremor registered at least a 4.0 magnitude on the Richter scale. State officials closed the Spirit Lake Information Center and several roads leading to the mountain.

Alex's house lost power again. Fortunately, his father had purchased the last generator in stock at the hardware store. The store clerk, who was so smug about the possible danger earlier, didn't smirk when told the supplies were needed in case of an eruption. In fact, the clerk admitted buying masks and goggles himself. Alex, of course, told Wendy, who took full credit for converting the clerk to "Team Volcano."

However, during one of the more serious quakes, the generator suddenly died, and the tremors kept coming in waves. Alex was worried a surge of water from Spirit Lake would flood the area. Wendy had written Alex that it might happen, but that the bigger concern would be the deadly clouds of ash that would cover the area and the streams of lava flowing out of the mountain. Alex wasn't sure which was worse.

More pictures crashed to the floor, and pots flew around the room. Alex and his family fled to the cellar. It was stocked with flashlights, blankets, water, and food. They had taken Wendy's advice and prepared their own emergency kits. Alex was relieved they didn't have to use the masks and goggles. The dry food was bad enough. Alex was not sure how much popcorn he could eat.

The quakes kept rolling, each one growing stronger. The larger quakes hit at least three times a day. Alex had promised Wendy he would record them, and he did. Smaller ones seemed to occur about every hour. Alex was glad that he and Wendy had never built their earthquake machine as it would be going crazy now. Alex's mother kept in touch with David, the geologist.

His team was using laser instruments to record what was happening. They were located six miles from the mountain. David was convinced that Mount St. Helens was going to erupt soon. He even stopped by Michael's house to remind him how dangerous it was for Michael to remain. Michael tried to shrug off the dangers, but David reported back that he was sure if the mountain blew, Michael would evacuate. This relieved Alex's worries. Now they just had to hope the helicopter could reach Michael in time, in case he didn't evacuate before the eruption. Alex began to feel like he was in the middle of a Jules Verne novel and was at the center of the Earth.

Alex's family began packing their "must-save" things in a large trunk. Alex tucked away his paintings. Though images of Smoky were stamped in his memory, he wanted his sketches and paintings. He also saved his copy of Thoreau's *Walden*. His mother packed away all their family photos and the silver her mother had left her. Alex's father added his Japanese art prints. Each added one family heirloom. Alex added his lava rock, while his mother contributed a brooch from her grandmother. It wasn't worth much, but Jenny had always loved the way the garnets had sparkled in the sunlight. Alex had called it the lava pin. Alex laughed as his father added the stuffed fish he had supposedly caught when he was Alex's age. No one knew if the story was true, but the fish had been hanging in his father's office for so long that the tale had become fact, whether it was fact or fiction. Packing their treasures had calmed the family. Wendy, of course, had told them it was a brilliant idea. She would do the same in Portland. Alex wasn't sure why Wendy was doing it from well outside the volcano zone. But he appreciated how his friend tried to make him feel like they were a team.

Then on March 27th, they woke to a pounding on their door. A member of the evacuation team announced that an official hazard watch had been issued. The Porter family dressed and immediately began loading the car with their "must-have" trunk. They stood on the porch nervously, unsure whether they should stay or go. As the family decided that they were still safe, an eruption of steam exploded from the summit. Alex checked his watch. It was noon but you couldn't tell from the darkened sky. Ash and steam rose from the cone into the air. Later, Alex would learn it had shot up around 6,000 feet and that the quake had registered 4.7 on the Richter scale leaving behind a 200-foot crater.

To Alex, the ash plume was a monstrous sight because what might follow could be much worse. Who knew if that was just the first blast? The family decided to evacuate, even though no such orders had been issued. David, the geologist, had assured them they were still in the safe zone, but the Porters voted unanimously to travel to Portland—after all, it was better to be cautious in matters of life and death.

Alex's father drove them nonstop at the speed limit to Portland to stay with Wendy and her family. Alex kept looking out the back window, thinking the quakes and ash would follow. He couldn't wait to report on the eruption. He knew Wendy would first be upset she hadn't experienced it, and then she'd have tons of questions. The only answers Alex would have would be how terrified he had been. He would have to admit his eyes were closed during most of the eruption. The huge plume of smoke had really freaked him out. *Sorry, Wendy.*

Once they were in Portland, Alex's mom kept in touch with David, and they learned that by March 31st, instruments were beginning to record volcanic tremors. Wendy explained that this meant the magma, the molten rock beneath Mount St. Helens, was on the move. A state of emergency had been declared in the area, and even though local schools were closed, Alex didn't feel like celebrating.

While the reports from David thrilled Wendy, they only made Alex more concerned about Michael. Although Alex knew it was hopeless, he tried to concentrate and send Michael mental messages to evacuate. He told Wendy what he was doing and expected her to laugh at him, but instead she calmly said that she would do the same.

CHAPTER 14

April lived up to its reputation as an odd weather month in the Pacific Northwest. On April 1st, plumes of steam and ash exploded out of the summit and were reported to reach a height of 20,000 feet. This was no April Fool's Day joke. Within two days, the crater expanded to 1,500 feet wide and about 300 feet deep. Alex's parents told Wendy's family that they might have to temporarily take up actual residence in Portland. Wendy was so concerned about her friend and his reaction to the news, she didn't even complain that she wasn't in the vicinity of Smoky to actually experience the volcano.

Then, late in the month, the earthquakes stopped. There were still minor tremors, but those were considered aftershocks—at least, according to volcano expert Wendy. With the situation quieter, the Porters returned home. Still, Alex felt they were marking time until the main event. Wendy had convinced her mother that if things were quiet for the rest of April, she could go to Alex's the second or third week in May. Wendy had said it could be an early birthday gift since her birthday was in June. As Alex and his family were leaving, he playfully punched Wendy and told her to be careful what she wished for.

Once home, Alex's family began the big clean up. Ash from the initial eruption was everywhere. Alex wondered if this wasn't even the main event, what would things be like after the big eruption?

When they were finished cleaning, Alex—with water, mask, goggles, and the walkie-talkie—went to check on Michael. It looked like a huge boulder had hit Michael's porch.

Its columns were tilting and the porch seemed to sway, but personally Michael claimed he was fine. Alex noticed that Michael didn't say anything about the windows that had shattered and were now boarded up. Michael's only complaint was that he was out of dry food, so Alex promised to bring him some the next day. Alex was more than happy to share the popcorn.

The rest of April remained quiet, but David the geologist reported that the laser equipment had detected changes in Mount St. Helens' profile. She was no longer the beauty she had once been. Bulges or swelling from the gushing of magma, or molten rock, were forming between the fissures. Wendy reported back that that was not a good sign, but she still planned on coming since the quakes had calmed down.

However, even though it was quiet, by late April the bulge appeared to be growing at a rate of five feet per day. Alex could tell that Wendy wanted to leap through the phone to get there, but she still had to wait until May. Meanwhile,

Alex focused on completing his painting of Mount St. Helens. He wanted to get everything perfect, as he knew the mountain—even if it did return to its former glory one day—would never be the same. The painting would capture his memories of Mount St. Helens before the eruption and that was the reason Alex was so committed to getting it right. He knew that when Wendy arrived, those images would return.

CHAPTER 15

Alex feared the ash from the earlier eruptions would never disappear. From his bike he'd left on the porch to the chest his family used to store water, everything seemed to be coated in thick ash. Some of it had even seeped inside the house. Alex's mother complained that her washer still didn't work right even though it had been a month since the major eruption. His father kept cleaning out the car filter and then simply just replaced it with a new one every week. He claimed the added expenses caused by the ash would send them all to the poor house.

Getting Michael to, at least, evacuate down the mountain to their house failed. Alex tried different strategies, including mentioning the well-being of Michael's cat. But Michael stood his ground, refusing to leave. Alex knew his mother objected to him spending time in Michael's lodge, which was directly in the path of a possible lava flow. Alex had even resorted to drawing lava flowing over Michael's house and sharing the picture of Pompeii that Wendy had sent, but Michael still was unmoved. *Stubborn, thy name is Michael,* Alex thought. Finally, Alex gave up. He talked with Wendy about it during their next phone call.

"I've tried everything, Wendy, and I can't get the old guy to budge," Alex moaned. "I don't know what to do. I've even painted horrible images of what would happen if he stayed." Alex took a deep breath.

"Did you tell him about Mount Vesuvius?" Wendy asked. She had sent Alex images of the casts of the dead from the nearby city of Pompeii. Wendy had thought the photos were gross and might trouble Michael, but according to Alex, they had failed to persuade Michael to move.

"Of course I told him about Vesuvius and Pompeii. I'm not an idiot," Alex replied. His voice showed frustration, and Wendy knew enough to back off.

"Okay, got it. Calm down," Wendy said in what she hoped was a reassuring voice.

"I am calm," Alex almost shouted back. *Yeah, right,* Wendy thought. *If that were calm, I'd hate to see you upset.* "Listen, I've gotta run," Alex said. "Catch you later." And with that, Alex hung up before he got another lecture on volcanoes or ideas about ways to get Michael to evacuate. Alex knew Wendy meant well, but sometimes she could be a little overbearing, and Alex was in no mood for her advice. Alex pounded the wall in frustration.

"Hey, don't take it out on the wall, kiddo," his mother warned as she walked past. "I'm sure Wendy was only trying to help."

"Yeah, right," Alex muttered as he trudged up to his room. He threw himself on his bed and tried to block out what was happening. He picked up a book by good old Thoreau, but even his author friend couldn't comfort Alex. Besides, he was sorry for being so abrupt with Wendy. He knew she'd only been trying to help. At the next opportunity, Alex would apologize. He didn't want a volcano to spoil their friendship. If Alex hadn't been so frustrated, he would have laughed at the absurdity of that remark, but a volcano was changing their relationship.

Meanwhile, back in Portland, Wendy stared at the phone. The dial tone turned to loud beeping noises. Wendy's mother took the receiver from her hand and put in back in its cradle.

"Look, pumpkin," her mother said. "Alex is just upset with the situation, not you. He's concerned he won't be able to save Michael. You know Michael is like a grandfather to him, and Alex wants to keep him safe. I think it would be helpful to just listen to him. He needs a good friend."

Wendy's mom patted her on the head and gave her a hug. Normally, Wendy would have rolled her eyes, muttered "Don't call me pumpkin," ducked out of the embrace, and commented sarcastically, "Really, ya think?!"—but this time her mother was right.

"I'll write him a letter since I can't visit," Wendy said, hoping that her remark might play on her mother's sympathy.

"Look, if it's still quiet and the experts think it's safe there next weekend, you can go," her mother promised after thinking long and hard before answering. "I'll call Jenny and check it out." Wendy wanted to pump the air with her fist and shout "YES!" but she knew better. Instead, she hugged her mother and quietly murmured, "Thanks." Her mother continued. "Write that letter to Alex. That will cheer him up and make him feel better. That's what good friends do." Wendy nodded and hurried to her room. Except for her possible visit, Wendy had no idea what she could say that would make Alex feel better.

One subject she wouldn't mention was another volcano, Krakatoa, in Asia. The impact of its eruption a hundred years ago was felt around the globe. Volcanic debris in the air lowered temperatures worldwide. Temporarily, sunrises and sunsets became even more colorful, and the sun and moon appeared to be a shade of blue-green. Although devastating, the volcano also inspired many artists. Wendy told Alex that a volcano had been the inspiration for Edvard Munch's classic painting, *The Scream.*

Courtesy, The Metropolitan Museum of Art

This was not the time to tell Alex that a volcano might inspire his painting. Instead, she might inform him about her not finishing last in a recent race at a school track meet. Yes, that might make him smile. Alex continually teased her that she always had her nose in a book and was unathletic. Wendy always just laughed, even though the remarks did sting a little. Besides, it wasn't like Alex was a star athlete, but he was an above average runner and soccer player. And, even though she did call him "Lone Wolf," he was a team player when he had to be.

Still, Wendy thought Alex liked the privacy of running best. Someday she'd ask him about his wish to be alone. Besides, her taking up track was a pretty "rad" idea. Wendy could mention that if old Smoky blew her top, at least she could escape without Alex's help. *Maybe not so very comforting,* Wendy thought as she chuckled. She did have to work on her people skills. Maybe she'd just mention the race and a joke about her competing in the Olympics. *Even better.* Being a good friend was not as easy as *Seventeen Magazine* made it out to be. No matter what, Wendy couldn't wait to see Alex and old Smoky.

CHAPTER 16

Alex arrived home from school and checked the mail. *Yes, a letter from Wendy.* He put it aside—it was probably just a list of volcanoes, stories about death and destruction, and estimates on when Smoky would blow. *Sorry pal, not in the mood,* Alex thought. However, once he was lying on his bed, it felt that some magical force was beckoning him to read the letter. Still, Alex hesitated. *Don't be a jerk, just read it.* Alex took his own advice and ripped open the envelope and began reading.

Hey Buddy.

 ○○○ Buddy? (I must have really made her feel bad; clearly, the girl is overcompensating.) Chill, Miss Volcanologist...although I'm glad I apologized for hanging up on you.

I was in an indoor race last weekend, and guess what? I didn't come in last.

○○○ Hey, good for you.

I know I won't be up to your speed....get it? But maybe we could go running when I'm there.

○○○ Cool idea.

It would be fun to run along the different paths.

○○○ It would, but I'm not sure we'd be allowed on them. But there are paths by the house. We just have to stay behind the fifteen-mile radius. (Wait until Wendy hears that. She'll blow faster and louder than old Smoky.)

I have made a decision. I think I am going to go to school in Iceland.

○○○ What, dudette?! That is bizarre, but then considering the source, maybe not. Don't expect me to board a plane and come visit. (Her obsessions last about a year at most. By the time college rolls around, Iceland will no longer be in her plans.)

It's called the "island of fire and ice." Iceland is made up of volcanoes.

　　⚬◯◯ I knew she couldn't resist talking about
　　　　　 volcanoes. (One of the interesting things
　　　　　 about Wendy is her fixations on things
　　　　　 and how much information she soaks up.
　　　　　 Encyclopedias were made for her.)

Did you know that was the reason Jules Verne had his explorers start their journey to the center of the Earth there? You know the book about the journey to the center of the Earth? By the way, the facts are all wrong!!!!! Jules Verne got a lot of future science right, like submarines and travel to the moon, but not to the center of the Earth. Of course, if he had the facts right, then the explorers could have never traveled to the center of the Earth. I guess that's what makes it science FICTION.

　　Anyway, you can study volcanoes in Iceland—not the center of the Earth. It's a paradise for volcanologists. As one report said, "It's one of the few places where earth, geology, and human history are connected to volcanoes."

　　⚬◯◯ Geesh, you sound like an encyclopedia.
　　　　　 (I know Wendy has an amazing memory and
　　　　　 can quote things she read months, even
　　　　　 years ago.)

　　Scientists there can measure and observe the tectonic plate movements. Cool, huh?

○⊂◯ I'd rather be like Monet and just sit in a
garden painting lilies, but to each his own,
right?

Well, enough about volcanoes. Have you been
watching any good TV? My mom FINALLY let me
watch *Saturday Night Live*. It's hilarious. Gilda
Radner is super funny. I love her Rosanna character. I
read that the character is based on a real newscaster.
And Gilda has curly hair just like me. My dad likes
Bill Murray, but I think the women are funnier. You
should check it out.

○⊂◯ I will. If your mom lets you watch it, I bet
mine will, too.

They also have neat musical groups and singers like
James Taylor and Paul Simon. My mom loves James
Taylor, and she kept telling me to be quiet while he
sang. I guess he's good, but I prefer Blondie and
Debbie Harry.

○⊂◯ Female singer, why am I not surprised.
Though she is good and even I like "Heart
of Glass."

Steve Martin has been on it. He's kind of funny, though
I must admit he sort of reminds me of your dad, until
he picks up a banjo. Jane Curtin does the news, and my
mom says she has a dry tone. I'm not sure what that
means, except that she says everything the same.

○◌◯ I think that's deadpan. (Even though Wendy
          laughs easily, she doesn't often get jokes.
          Too much a science dweeb. Not that I'm
          much better.)

And to paraphrase *Saturday Night Live*, that's about
all the news that is fit to print from Portland.

○◌◯ Funny, Wendy.

     OK. Let's get it out there. I know you're upset
about Michael, but dude, there is NOTHING you
can do. This, as our moms would say, is one of those
decisions that is out of our control. It's not great or
cool, but that's the skinny. So don't be an airhead and
let it go, and focus on other things. How's the painting?
It must be finished by now. I can't wait to see it. I
bet it's awesome.

○◌◯ It is, if I do say so myself.

     And the best part is that next weekend, I'll be there
to drive you crazy so you won't have any time to be
frustrated or feel down.

○◌◯ You will drive me crazy, but I can't wait.

     See you soon,
     Wendy, future Icelandic villager

Alex carefully put the letter back in the envelope and added it to the mountain of others. *Well, at least that mountain won't erupt.* But the mountain did cave in and topple over. Laughing, Alex put the mountain back together. *We can do the same thing with old Smoky. I wonder how long it would take.* Wendy would know. For once, Alex was glad Wendy was an expert on volcanoes.

CHAPTER 17

Wendy boarded the bus and waved good-bye to her mother. She had promised to listen to Alex's mother and not wander off on her own anywhere near the mountain. Her mother had repeated it three times, and each time Wendy had not rolled her eyes, crossed her fingers, or anything else. She had quietly answered, "Yes, Mom." Finally, her mother had believed her. Wendy had no intention of wandering off on her own, *but* she would get as close to Smoky as she could safely. Wendy was so excited that she was jumping up and down as if she had just won a relay race.

A woman sitting across the aisle glanced at her several times. Finally, she asked Wendy,

"Are you all right, dear? You seem a little nervous."

Wendy tried to still her legs and calm down. "Yes, I'm fine. I'm just terribly excited to see my friend. It's been quite a while since we last visited."

Where did that voice come from? Wendy wondered. *I sound like something out of one of those Jane Austen novels my mother reads.* Her mother had tried to share them with Wendy, but she preferred her books on volcanoes. Even Alex's mother had said the Austen books were a fun read, but at least she understood Wendy's attraction to science texts. Wendy loved that she could discuss science with her Aunt Jenny and she didn't look at her oddly as Alex and her mother did.

In fact, Wendy thought in some ways Alex was more like her mother, sort of a dreamer and an artist, even though she was a lawyer who relied more on logic than emotion. She kept that side of her personality hidden in public. Wendy was more like Alex's mother, who also loved science. The two women had been friends for years, so it was not surprising that Alex and Wendy became close friends as well.

"Where is your friend?" Wendy snapped back to reality.

She turned to the woman and answered, "He lives near Mount St. Helens."

"Oh, isn't that where the volcano is located?" the woman asked. " I recently heard about it on the news." She looked concerned.

"Yes, it is, but the volcano has been quiet for two weeks now, and some scientists think it may have gone dormant, though I don't agree with them or that theory," Wendy answered. The woman smiled at Wendy, but Wendy could tell the poor woman was flustered and didn't know quite what to say. Wendy thought of telling the woman that girls could love science and be good at it, too, but then she heard Alex's voice in her head. *Spare the woman your lecture, Wendy; she's just trying to be nice, so calm down and be friendly.*

"I love volcanoes," Wendy grinned. She hoped that would answer any questions the woman had. The woman nodded and muttered, "That's nice, dear," and then she returned to her knitting. *End of conversation,* Wendy thought. *So much for Alex's advice; I tried.*

Shrugging, Wendy pulled out her book on Krakatoa and read how the ash from the volcano in Indonesia had polluted the atmosphere all around the Earth. Wendy found the idea of the sunsets and sunrises changing colors fascinating. *How could Alex not love this?* Wendy wondered what color green they had been and how long the skies had been dark. The aftereffects had been felt thousands of miles away and affected many people who had never even heard of Krakatoa.

Wendy wondered if that is what would happen when Smoky finally exploded. Her thoughts quickly turned to Michael. Alex was right to be worried about Michael and his foolish decision not to be evacuated. *We have to get him out of there,* Wendy thought. The woman cleared her throat, and Wendy wondered if she had been talking out loud. Sometimes when she was in the zone, she did. Just in case, Wendy smiled at the woman one more time. *I'm not crazy.* Wendy hoped her thoughts reached the woman. She turned back to her book and got caught up in the tale of Krakatoa.

The similarities between it and Smoky were eerie. In some ways, Krakatoa was more like Mount St. Helens than Vesuvius was. It was almost like she was reading about the future. She just had to substitute Krakatoa with Smoky. Just like Smoky, ash clouds had appeared above the mountain before the eruption. A German ship observed the ash clouds. And just like the area around Smoky, for the next two months, ships reported experiencing thunderous noises and dense cloud cover. Wendy shivered as she read, but she couldn't stop herself from reading.

People had held festivals celebrating the fireworks in the night sky. Well, that was one big difference. Wendy knew it was a sure bet that the people around Mount St. Helens weren't celebrating. It was more likely that they were doing what Alex's family was—packing up their treasures and proofing their houses so that when the ash rained down on them, it wouldn't get in the house. But Wendy wasn't sure that could really be prevented. It seemed to Wendy that the ash storm would probably be more like the Dust Bowl, where dust storms buried everything in dust and crept into houses, no matter how much people tried to seal windows and doors. One thing was for sure, they had to get Michael off the mountain before it was too late.

Thinking about Smoky and what was most likely going to happen, Wendy wasn't sure if she was scared or excited. She knew Alex was scared and worried. Wendy decided that reading about Krakatoa probably wasn't the best idea on the planet, so she slammed her book shut and shoved it into her backpack. The old woman knitted faster. Wendy closed her eyes and drifted off to sleep.

Soon Wendy and Alex were running along the paths of Smoky, but before they could reach Alex's house, the sky turned black and ash poured down on them. It seared their faces and Wendy felt like she was burning up. Alex looked like a molten statue and appeared to be melting. The two of them were doomed and there was no escape. Wendy cried out, "No, Alex! We're too late for Smoky!" A hand bore down on Wendy and she felt herself being shaken. Suddenly, Wendy's eyes flew open.

It was the woman trying to wake her. "You were having a nightmare, dear. Sorry I had to shake you, but you were whispering something about Smoky and Alex." The woman looked concerned. "Thank you," Wendy said. "I was having a bad dream about volcanoes. I think I read too much about them." She smiled at the woman and tried to look normal. *I'm still not crazy.* "Well, I'm sure your friend Alex and his pet Smoky are fine," the woman said.

The woman shook her head and returned to her knitting. Wendy nodded and tried not to giggle. *Alex, my man, where are you when I need you?* In a way, Smoky was like a pet to Alex, but the mountain wasn't fine.

For the rest of the journey, Wendy kept her mind on other things and just stared out the window. The bus driver announced the Nighthawk stop, and Wendy gathered up her backpack and turned to the woman. "Have a wonderful trip," she said to the woman.

"You, too, dear," the woman replied. Smiling one last time at the woman, Wendy left the bus.

Once in the open air, Wendy breathed a sigh of relief. At last she was where she was meant to be. Wendy looked around in vain for Alex and his parents. She hoped that Smoky had not yet erupted. But Wendy looked up at the sky and it was blue—just like Lake Spirit—and there was not a cloud visible either. She walked over to one of the benches, set her backpack down, and waited. Wendy kept monitoring the sky, but it remained blue and clear. *So far, so good,* she thought.

Moments later, Alex and his mother arrived. Alex bounded from the car and ran over to her. "Hi, sorry, we're late, but Mom had to go and explain why hikes have been canceled on Smoky. You'd think people would watch the news and know what was going on. But I guess some thought that since Smoky hadn't erupted and had been quiet, the danger was over and it was safe to hike near the summit. We're even getting tourists who are camping all around the mountain, waiting to see Smoky blow her top. They are plain foolish." Alex realized he might have gone too far, as Wendy would love to camp nearby when Smoky erupted. Quickly, he tried to cover himself. "I wish you had been there so you could spout some facts at them! The people wouldn't believe Mom, so it took longer than we thought to convince them that it was chancy to hike Smoky."

Alex was relieved when Wendy laughed and agreed, "I certainly could have told them what was happening." They headed to the car.

"So people like you and me can't go near the mountain?" Wendy asked, in a voice that made it clear she was not going to like the answer.

Alex took a deep breath. "No, not really. They moved out everyone who lived within a fifteen-mile radius. I thought I had told you." Alex was almost positive he had, but maybe not. Wendy was notorious for only hearing what she wanted. And with Smoky, she was like a dog with a bone and wouldn't give up on what she planned. Still, Alex felt sorry for his friend, who wanted to not only see but experience the eruption. "Sorry," he said.

Wendy nodded. In a way, Alex was apologizing because she couldn't move closer to the volcano. She had hoped that since the area around Smoky had been calm, the barrier might have been abandoned, but no such luck. "It is what it is," Wendy proclaimed in a disappointed voice.

"Hey, we can hike near there tomorrow and you can still get some good photos," Alex said. "You brought your camera, right?"

"Of course," Wendy said, rolling her eyes. "What kind of a volcanologist would I be if I wasn't prepared to photograph what happens? Unlike some people, who shall remain nameless, I am always prepared." Striking a conquering pose, Wendy hoisted her backpack on her shoulders and walked over to Alex's mother.

Alex wanted to comment "Yeah, you're a regular Boy Scout," but he didn't. There was no sense in starting the visit off on a bad foot. He could tell Wendy was cranky and wanted her to be in a good mood. He needed his friend's help to work out a solution to what Alex and his family now referred to as the "Michael problem."

"Come on, guys, let's go," Mrs. Porter said. "I'm sure you want to explore." She could read Wendy's mind. They all got in the car and drove back to Alex's house. Normally, good old Smoky seemed close to the house, almost as if you could touch her. But for some reason, today she looked miles away—more like the moon, distant and forbidding—than a friendly neighbor.

The car pulled into the driveway, and Alex and Wendy raced into the house. Alex's mother just laughed at their youthful energy. By the time she reached the front door, Wendy had already dropped her backpack in the guest room and had her camera out. Alex barely had time to grab his sketchpad and box of pencils. Alex's mother reminded him to take the walkie-talkie with them, and he grabbed it from the hall bench as the two ran out. "Be home for supper," Alex's mother called, but she doubted that they heard her. Smoky had already captured the two adventurers in her web.

CHAPTER 18

As they approached the barrier, Alex noticed that Wendy did not complain about their trek and had kept up with his brisk pace. "Wow, running track has paid off for you," Alex commented as they rested under a fir tree.

Wendy nodded. "Yeah, I'll never be a track star, but at least I can keep up with you now," she said. "And having good boots helps, too."

Alex looked at Wendy's sturdy footwear designed to protect her feet. Wendy also wore knee-length hiking socks, but Alex didn't comment on their bold design, bright red with a border of green leaves. Wendy smirked when she saw Alex look at her socks and then looked away.

"Hey, you know me," Wendy beamed. "I like a dash of style."

Alex simply nodded. *Red hair, red socks, and fiery personality, I should call her "Flame Girl,"* Alex thought.

Wendy pulled out her camera, focusing on a hemlock tree farther up the mountain and adjusting her lens. "Will you be able to get shots of the bulge in the mountain caused by the pressure of the molten rock under the surface?" Alex asked. He doubted she could, as they were not yet at the barrier.

But Wendy shrugged. "I probably can. This lens is pretty powerful. My mom got it for me and I've been practicing taking shots with it." Wendy clicked a few shots and then put the cap back on her lens. "Let's go."

The two continued up the mountain to the barrier. Enjoying the peace and tranquility, neither spoke. Alex wondered how long this experience would continue. On the other hand, Wendy hoped that if the eruption were to happen, it would happen while she was there. She wasn't sure she could return next weekend, and Wendy was confident Smoky was going to erupt soon. But since her backpack with the masks, gloves, and other eruption essentials had been left behind, she hoped it wasn't today.

Finally, the two reached the barrier, which consisted of yellow tape strung along wooden road blocks. No one in authority, not a lawman or even a forest ranger, was around to question their presence. The barrier had been haphazardly put together. In some places, there were metal "fences." Alex wondered how Wendy would react to what was clearly a boundary. Wendy openly objected to being limited in any way. When they first became good friends, Wendy had worked hard at ripping down what she called any "walls" between them. He hoped she would not rip down the barrier but stay behind it. *Oh well, cross that barrier when I get to it,* Alex smiled at his joke.

Wendy immediately checked if there was any opening they could sneak through, but Alex put a hand on her shoulder. "Don't even think about it,

Wendy. I promised my mom we would stay behind the barrier, and we're keeping that promise. That's the only reason she let us come up here."

"You're such a Goody Two-shoes," Wendy teased, but in some ways she was relieved Alex was so responsible. His calming influence held her more thoughtless impulses in check, so they worked well as a balancing act.

However, the two went around a bend where Alex thought they might have a better view of Smoky. "This seems a little better," he said.

"It is, thanks," Wendy said as she resumed taking pictures. Her mouth turned down and her face looked determined as she concentrated on her shots. She kept shooting and Alex relaxed, knowing she wouldn't go bounding up the mountain past the barrier. Besides, the scientists and rangers patrolled the area, so it was unlikely Wendy could sneak past the barrier without being spotted eventually. Alex opened his pad and started to sketch. He drew out the cone and drew in a wide crater. He wasn't sure how accurate his drawing was, but he knew that since the blast in March, the top was no longer the familiar snowcapped peak. Wendy wandered by and peered over his shoulder. "I think the crater needs to be a little wider, and there wouldn't be that much snow left on the mountain since that blast in March would have melted it," she said. "The geologists said it was about 1,300 feet wide, plus there are two giant cracks across the summit."

"Thanks, Miss Know-it All," Alex said.

Wendy laughed, "Hey, just want it to be accurate."

Alex chuckled, erased what he had sketched, and drew the crater wider and added two large cracks. "Is this better?"

Wendy studied the sketch. "Yup, much better."

Alex drew a few evergreens and added a golden eagle circling the mountain. He had never actually seen an eagle up close so he used his imagination. He shared the sketch with Wendy, who held back from telling him that all birds had most likely left the mountain.

"Looks good," she said.

Satisfied, Alex closed his pad and put his pencils away. If it were anyone else commenting on his work, Alex probably would have become defensive. But he realized Wendy was just being honest and had good intentions, though she still could get on his nerves. Alex decided to tackle "the elephant in the room," as Michael might say. "So, when does the great volcano expert and fortune teller think the eruption will happen?" he asked, unsure if he really wanted Wendy to answer.

Wendy handled her camera as if it were a crystal ball. "Well, oh foolish one, I see a huge cloud that blackens the sky. Fire reigns down. It will happen soon."

"I could have made that prediction," Alex taunted. "Honestly, you know that eruptions are unpredictable, but from the different reports that you and your mom shared from the scientists, it can occur any time now," Wendy declared authoritatively.

"Boom!" Alex yelled in Wendy's ear.

"Funny, dork, funny," Wendy retorted. "Come on, let's head back. I have all the pictures I need for now. We can come up early tomorrow, and I'll shoot another roll of film."

Alex groaned. "How early is early?" he asked. Wendy chuckled. It would be fun to irritate Alex by forcing him to rise at the crack of dawn.

"Oh, let's say sunrise," she smirked. Alex shook his head, but he knew he'd probably be up and about anyway. Lately, he hadn't been able to sleep late with all that was happening.

"Should we stop and see Michael?" Wendy asked. She braced herself for a sarcastic reply from Alex, but he just nodded his head and said, "Yeah, you can tell him that Smoky is going to erupt any moment and if he wants to survive, he had better get himself off the mountain." Michael's place was just within the barrier space, and the rangers had basically given up trying to convince Michael to evacuate. "My mom worked out a kind of plan with the rescue team, and if Michael hasn't left by the time Smoky blows, they will immediately fly in to rescue him."

"Can we fly in with them?" Wendy asked, looking so hopeful that Alex didn't have the heart (or courage) to disappoint her. "Uhm, maybe. We'd have to get their permission and stuff," Alex fumbled with his reply.

"I'm sure your mom will work it out so we can," Wendy responded. Alex sighed. *Gee, Wendy, nothing like applying pressure.* The two hiked over to Michael's. As they approached, Michael rose from his seat and waved. Dusty was nestled at his feet. Wendy snapped a couple of photos of Michael and his house. Wendy knew that once Smoky blew, the lodge would probably be severely damaged if not destroyed. Then Wendy threw back her shoulders; she was determined that this time she'd convince Michael to evacuate. Alex followed Wendy quietly, having recognized her "take no prisoners" mood.

"Hey, Van Gogh and volcano girl, how goes it?" Michael asked.

"We're fine," Wendy replied. She bent down to pet the cat. "So you know that animals sense when something in nature is wrong and a disaster is about to happen."

Alex stared at Wendy. *What was she babbling about?*

"I do. And you'll notice how silent 'my girl' is. I think the deer, elk, and other wildlife are moving away," Michael replied.

"You should join them," Wendy said bluntly. Alex held his breath.

Michael laughed. "You always speak your mind," he said. "I like an independent person."

Wendy smiled at the compliment and then turned serious. "I mean it."

"I know you do, and you'll both be relieved to learn that I've agreed to leave when 'my girl' blows her top," Michael said, smiling at their surprised faces. "Alex, your mom has made arrangements to get me out of here. A helicopter can land in the field near the lodge, and I promise to be on it and out of here when it's safe to evacuate. One thing, though. I'd feel a lot more comfortable if you were on that helicopter, too."

"We will be. It's a promise. But, you don't think you should leave right now?" Alex pressed. He knew it was hopeless to ask, but felt he had to try. Wendy drew her finger across her throat signaling Alex not to force the issue.

"Who knows when she will explode? Then again, she might not," Michael said, holding up his hand to Wendy. "I know you don't believe that, but I'm staying as long as I can."

"Okay," Alex replied. It was a compromise, and Alex wished Michael would come home with him now. But it was preferable to Michael vowing not to leave under any circumstances.

"Do you two have time for a cup of tea?" Michael asked.

"No, I think we better get back," Alex said, and just as he answered Michael, the walkie-talkie squawked. It was Alex's mother telling them it was time to get home. The two bid good-bye to Michael. Wendy patted the cat once more, and the two started off to Alex's house.

"Well, that's a relief," Wendy concluded.

"Yeah, but..." Alex began.

But Wendy interrupted. "Look, Alex, you did the best you could and at least he's agreed to evacuate. You did great." Wendy gave Alex a mock salute.

"Fine," Alex said, hiding a smile. Words of encouragement from a friend like Wendy were special.

During the hike back, Alex reminded Wendy to work how she watched *Saturday Night Live* into their conversation that night to see how his parents would react. Wendy agreed. The two went on about their favorite TV shows, leaving thoughts of Smoky behind, for a few moments at least.

When they reached Alex's house, his father told them to wash up and then come downstairs for supper.

"Something smells good!" Wendy exclaimed.

Alex nodded in agreement. His father knew his way around a kitchen. Wendy looked forward to the meals Alex's father whipped up, unlike at home, where she often had to settle for take-out food or frozen dinners due to her parents' busy work schedules. Wendy loved pizza and Chinese food, but a home-cooked meal was a welcomed treat.

The four sat down to a meal of rainbow trout from the waters around Spirit Lake, mashed potatoes, and green peas. "This is delish," Wendy said between mouthfuls. "Did you catch this fish yourself, Mr. Porter?"

"No, I bought it from one of the protesters a while back and froze it. Just defrosted it today and fried it." Alex's father admitted sheepishly.

Alex changed the subject. He wiggled his eyebrows to remind Wendy of their agreement to test his parents' knowledge of late night TV.

"Say, do you guys watch *Saturday Night Live*?" Wendy asked. Alex knew she was trying to act innocently like the two had never discussed the show. But like Alex, Wendy was not always a convincing actress. But to Alex's surprise, her ploy worked.

Alex's parents laughed. "Why, should we?"

Wendy seized the opportunity to discuss the TV show. "Well, you should. It's so b-a-d."

"Bad?" Alex's father raised his eyebrows.

"That means good, Dad," Alex replied.

"I realize that," his father said not quite convincingly.

Alex laughed, knowing full well that his father probably didn't know.

His mother smiled. "I do hear it's hilarious. Who's your favorite on the show, Wendy?"

"I love Gilda Radner. She's funny, she has curly hair, and she's awesome!" Wendy exclaimed. "I'm her number-one fan."

"No, how do you really feel?" Alex smirked.

"Watch it, airhead," Wendy retorted.

Alex's mother cleared her throat, and Alex and Wendy immediately stopped their bickering, even if it was good-natured.

"So, could we watch the show?" Alex asked.

"Don't you want to get up at the crack of dawn tomorrow?" Alex's mother asked with one eyebrow raised. She knew Alex was not a morning person.

"Ugh, yeah," Alex said, disappointed. "How about just the opening monologue?" he replied.

Alex gave Wendy a thumbs-up. *Good call,* she thought. "We'll do the dishes and rest before the show," Alex promised.

"That sounds fair," Alex's father said. His mother agreed.

"Yes!" Alex and Wendy shouted as they high-fived each other.

"You can start the cleanup right after dessert," Alex's father said. "Who wants banana cream pie?" Alex and Wendy raised their hands, and Mr. Porter fetched dessert.

Between mouthfuls, Wendy chattered about her favorite skits. Then, shooting Alex a look, Wendy quietly mentioned that her favorite guest host was Steve Martin. She looked over at Alex's father. *Subtle, Wendy, subtle...NOT,* Alex thought. Alex's father said that he had heard Steve Martin was a funny guy.

"Doesn't he play the banjo?" Alex's mother asked. Wendy nodded.

"You know, I played the banjo in college," Alex's father said.

Wendy looked at Alex and mouthed the words, "I told you."

Alex's mother shook her head saying, "I don't remember much about that."

"Well, it was short-lived," Alex's father responded. "Maybe I should take it up again." No one was sure how to respond, so they remained silent. Alex grinned. None of them had even mentioned Smoky or Michael. Instead, everyone looked forward to watching television that night but not the news.

Later that evening, however, Wendy dreamed about Gilda Radner doing a newscast from Mount St. Helens, her hair on fire with smoke surrounding her. Wendy woke and wondered if Alex was having a nightmare, too. She got up and went to the bedroom window. It was a clear night, though no stars were visible. *Not a good sign*, thought Wendy as she crawled back into bed. Even though Wendy had longed to experience a volcanic eruption, she now hoped tomorrow would be peaceful.

CHAPTER 19

Wendy groaned as the alarm buzzed at six o'clock that morning. She hit the snooze button and closed her eyes, then she remembered her dream. Wendy opened her eyes and felt her hair. Still red, still there. *Whew.*

Pulling the covers over her head, Wendy was starting to drift back to sleep when Alex knocked on her door. "Come on, Sleeping Beauty, time to rise and shine."

"Get a life, Mr. Perky," Wendy moaned. *What was with Alex?* He had never been a morning person, so who was that cheery guy? Wendy got up and made her way to the bathroom, where she doused her faced with warm water and brushed her teeth. Feeling more human, she dressed and went downstairs.

Alex was drinking orange juice. She approached him from behind and grabbed his shoulders. "Who are you and what have you done with the real Alex?" she asked.

"I was wondering the same thing," Alex's mother said.

Alex laughed. "Hey, it's leftover from last night. *Saturday Night Live* was hilarious, and it left me in a good mood."

"Wish I could say the same," Wendy said as she buttered her toast. "I dreamed Gilda Radner was doing a newscast from Smoky and was on fire. Not pretty. I'm surprised you didn't have nightmares, too."

"Nope, not me," Alex shrugged.

"Well, let's pack our stuff and go," Wendy said. She had every intention of bringing her volcano emergency kit.

"Okay, Commander Wendy." Alex saluted Wendy and she playfully punched him.

"Not funny," she said. But the two returned upstairs to prepare for their hike. Wendy replaced the books in her backpack with volcano emergency essentials: masks, a rope, a flashlight, gloves, and a hat. She had added a long, sturdy rope to grasp on the trail if necessary so the two wouldn't be separated. Even though it was predicted to be a warm day, Wendy wore a long-sleeved shirt and long pants that she could tuck into her socks. Just in case Smoky blew, Wendy was going to be covered, literally.

Alex was wearing a T-shirt and shorts, but Wendy made him change to clothes that offered more protection against the elements. At first, Alex refused, but then decided Wendy may be right. It was something he hated to admit, but, as always, it was better to be cautious.

"Don't forget your walkie-talkie," Alex's mother reminded them. Alex put it in Wendy's backpack. Once all the essentials were packed, Wendy and Alex grabbed an orange muffin to eat on the hike to the barrier.

On the trip up the mountain, Wendy didn't complain about Alex's pace once. *Her running track was really paying off,* Alex thought.

Wendy, of course, was unaware of this, as she was focused on recording their every move. *Geesh, you'd think we were part of a National Geographic special and not two kids on a hike,* Alex thought. Still, Alex was glad Wendy was taking so many photos. Once Smoky blew her top, the surrounding area would look very different.

Alex and Wendy reached the barrier beyond which they could not pass at 7:30, at least according to Wendy's watch. She carefully placed the roll of shot film in her pocket and then loaded another roll into her camera. She looked up at the sun high in the clear sky. To be safe, Wendy took out her hat but then put it back. It was too hot and too glorious a morning to be covered up! All was well. Alex calmly rested on a large rock. He gazed over at Smoky and wondered how long she'd be the beauty he loved. *And what will happen to Spirit Lake?* Alex put those thoughts aside and enjoyed the sun's winter rays caressing his face.

Wendy, however, was a whirling dervish. She set about taking more pictures. "I wish we could get closer," Wendy complained as she tried climbing a tree to get a better shot of the top of the mountain. It didn't work, so Wendy climbed down feeling frustrated. She stared at the barrier wishing it away.

Alex draped his arm on her shoulder. "Don't even think about it. We are not going any higher."

Wendy agreed, though she still was thinking of ways to go even farther up the mountain. Sighing, she realized that Alex was right and settled into taking shots of the trees and the mountain from where they were positioned. "It is a beautiful morning," Wendy commented. "These will make great 'before' photographs."

A jarring noise caused the two to look up. Fortunately, it was just a helicopter buzzing overhead.

"I'll bet they are getting some cool photos," Wendy said. Clearly, she wished they were in the chopper. "I don't suppose your mom knows the pilot, does she?"

Alex shook his head. Wendy never gave up. *Like a dog with a bone.*

He responded, "We can ask my mom when we get back. She knows some of the pilots. She made a deal with someone named P.T. to fly in and evacuate Michael when Smoky blows. Besides, they might also be practicing runs for emergency airlifts when the time comes."

"It would be dynamite if your mom could get me on a chopper," Wendy said.

With her determination and cunning, Alex believed Wendy would figure out a way to board a helicopter. He felt sorry for any pilot, including P.T., who stood in her way!

The two stared at Mount St. Helens in what Wendy's mom called "companionable silence," that is, sitting comfortably with one another without the need to speak. Nothing was happening, but then, after a few minutes, the silence became eerie. Except for insects, there were no normal sounds of wildlife. No birds were singing or even flying near them. Alex felt like he was alone in the dark in a horror movie, and sensed Wendy felt the same way.

As if reading his mind, Wendy turned to Alex and said, "It's kind of creepy, huh?"

Alex nodded and asked, "What time is it?"

Wendy looked at her watch. "It's 8:27. Maybe we should head back?"

Alex agreed and took a last close-up look at Smoky. He wondered how seriously the eruption, when it comes, would damage the area. Wendy remarked that afterward, it could take ten years or longer for things to return to normal.

Both were now anxious to leave the mountain. They could sense the old girl rumbling. Wendy took a few last shots of Smoky and then hung the camera around her neck. She only had two shots left on the roll, and as Alex would say, the Boy Scout in her wanted to be prepared in case there was something else to record. Wendy checked her supplies in the backpack and then hoisted it up. It was more cumbersome than heavy. If they had to run, it would be best to leave it behind. Wendy had a nagging feeling that they should start moving. She said nothing because she didn't want Alex to call her a fortune teller or a psychic.

As Wendy turned to tell Alex to pick up the pace, the ground suddenly moved. At first, Wendy thought she had imagined the tremor, but she was sure that the trees had swayed and nearby rocks shifted. The tremors were real. Wendy knew that tremors often happened immediately before an eruption. She glanced at Mount St. Helens. It still looked peaceful. However, Wendy made sure her camera was ready to snap a photo in case that scene changed. There was no way she'd miss the explosion. Still, Wendy wondered if it was real. After all, Alex always said she had a wild imagination.

"Tremor?" she asked hesitantly. Wendy was almost afraid to say the word aloud. She glanced over at Alex for confirmation. Sure enough, he looked nervous. Alex reminded Wendy of a deer caught in headlights. Wendy turned to Smoky and fired off one more photo. "Forget your photos; that was a bad one," Alex declared. "Come on, put the camera away and let's get going. We've got no time to lose."

The pair began to move when the earth shifted violently. They thought the earth might open and swallow them, but it didn't. Trees cracked and splintered around them. It sounded like gunfire, and Wendy and Alex had the urge to duck and hit the ground. Wendy glanced at her watch again. It was 8:32. A sudden movement knocked them both to the ground. "This is it!" Wendy cried. Mount St. Helens was finally erupting. Alex covered his ears. Now noise was greater, like cannons firing. Boom, boom, boom! A tower of ash plumed up from the mountain.

Instinctively, Wendy turned and took her last photo. With shaking hands, she ripped the roll of film from the camera and put it in her pocket. She shoved her camera into her backpack.

Alex grabbed the walkie-talkie. "We're on our way home!" he yelled, hitching it to his pants and heading down the path. Neither were sure if the message was received. But they hoped it wouldn't be their last. Wendy turned away from the erupting mountain and quickly followed Alex.

The two felt the wind gaining strength. Clouds of ash filled the sky, and ash flakes began raining down on them. Wendy couldn't remember how long it had taken them to climb to the barrier, but she knew they had less time to escape serious injury. A clock started ticking in Wendy's head, signaling how much time they had left. Instinctively, she threw down her backpack and opened it. She shouted at Alex to halt.

Fumbling, Wendy removed the masks and tossed one to Alex. Terrified, the two hurriedly put them on. The sky was turning ink black as the ash began to fall more intensely. It was like fleeing a burning blizzard. Around them more tree branches were cracking and falling. It was as if the trees on the mountain were being cut for lumber all at once. The two prayed that the fallen trees did not completely block their path. Alex feared the path being turned into an obstacle course that he and Wendy couldn't finish.

Wendy pulled out the rope. She tied it around her waist and threw the other end to Alex. He also fastened it around his midsection. Without speaking, the two continued their trek home and, hopefully, to safety. The burning ash raining down became hotter and heavier with each step they took. As the wind intensified, more ash blanketed the area. The two could barely walk, let alone run. Would they be able to make it out? Or would the ash bury them forever? One thing was certain—Alex was glad to have Wendy along. Her idea of tying them together could save both of their lives. Alex was no longer the lone wolf.

CHAPTER 20

Alex and Wendy pressed on, driven by Wendy's internal clock. Her heart pounded and echoed in her ears. Alex turned to speak but in all the chaos knew it would be useless. He used hand signals to direct Wendy to move faster. Wendy nodded. The two moved as quickly as possible under the dire conditions. They had trouble breathing, so their pace slowed. Between the wood debris crashing down and the ash storm surrounding them, running was impossible even if they had the strength. It felt like they were walking in steaming hot water.

Behind them, more trees just burst apart and tumbled down. Rocks seemed to shatter.

Breathing through the masks was difficult as the ash grew thicker. It was like being caught in a blizzard of hot, searing flakes. The ash burned holes in Alex's shirt, but there was little time to brush them all off. It was hard to coordinate their moves while tied together. Still, neither wanted to undo the rope out of fear that one of them would get lost or—even worse—left behind. Wanting to experience a volcanic eruption was one thing, but the reality of the event was just too terrifying. Alex tried to stay calm and kept telling himself that he knew every turn in the path by heart as he led Wendy to safety. But all he could do was place one foot in front of the other and hope they remained on the faint trail and could avoid the fallen trees. Alex kept going forward, his head tucked down and his eyes blinking wildly. He wondered how long Wendy could keep up with him. Hopefully, Wendy didn't realize how terrified and helpless he really felt.

Wendy glanced back at the mountain and didn't spot a branch that had just fallen across the trail. Wendy toppled headfirst and, grabbing the rope as she tumbled, pulled Alex down with her. She bounced back up, but as she took a step forward, searing pain shot through her left leg. Her ankle was injured, but there was no choice—Wendy had to proceed or they'd perish. Alex helped her up and coaxed her on, but she couldn't hear him.

Wendy leaned on Alex to get her bearings. She tried to inhale deeply, but ash filled her lungs. They'd never reach safety if Alex had to carry her. Alex flashed a "thumbs-up" signal, and Wendy nodded. They started off again. Sweating and scared, Wendy just kept moving forward, her eyes glued to the ground. She couldn't afford another misstep, despite the throbbing pain in her ankle. The great adventure had turned into a nightmare.

The air radiated intense heat like a firestorm. Gritting her teeth, Wendy plowed ahead. *You can do it, girl,* she repeated to herself. Alex was ahead, ready to act if she fell again, but another accident might mean she wouldn't be able to move at all. Wendy thought about how her teammates had cheered her on during her school races. She hadn't come close to winning any meets, but she had finished every race. Wendy kept summoning memories of her track squad cheering her on. It almost made her forget the pain. This was one race she had to finish.

Wendy felt like her lungs were about to burst, but there was no time to stop again. They had to keep moving. Their surroundings grew darker, and Wendy pulled out her flashlight. She tried to turn it on, but with the heavy ash falling, it was useless. Alex signaled her to just drop it. Alex knew the path and could lead them to safety— at least that was the plan. She dropped the flashlight and kept going. Wendy relied on Alex's sense of direction because she could barely see more than a foot in front of her, even with her head down. She could smell her red hair being singed and regretted not taking her hat with her, but it was too late to worry about that now. Wendy brushed hot ash off her cheek, ignoring the burning sensation.

As much as she tried to avoid it, her internal clock kept ticking. In her gut, Wendy knew they were running out of time. Somewhere Wendy had read that, based on the present conditions, they had about ten minutes to reach safety before the lava would flow down the mountain and overtake them. Despite her knowledge of volcanoes, she wondered if her estimate was accurate. Wendy glanced at her watch, which was coated with ash. It seemed like they had run a marathon down the mountain, but it had been only a few minutes. In front of her, Alex wheezed. He wanted to rip off his mask but knew he needed it to breathe. Still, even with the mask in place, Alex could still taste ash. The floating ash was like a vast, quickly moving fog from which there seemed to be no escape.

The gritty ash became thicker and heavier with each passing minute. The path began to disappear completely under the ash. The crashing trees and rocks continued to echo behind them. Alex's feared that either a tree limb would fall on them or debris would slide down the hill and roll over them.

Logging was always a presence in Alex's life. As long as he could remember, he had seen logs rolling down hills and floating in waterways to nearby sawmills. Now he pictured the evergreens doing the same. Alex winced at the thought of being crushed by the very evergreens he loved so much. He dismissed such thoughts and focused on following the path. One misstep could mean the end of both of them. He and Wendy could end up like those victims in ancient Pompeii who turned into deadly statues from the falling ash. Alex wished Wendy had never shared those images with him.

Wendy realized the ice from the summit of the mountain must have melted by now, creating hot streams. Lava would be pouring out of the crater, toppling trees, and crushing and burning anything in its path. Wendy suddenly halted. Alex turned toward her and pulled on the rope.

"Come on, Wendy, we have to keep going!" he shouted, his throat raw.

But Wendy just stood there, looking like one of those ash statues. Alex tugged on the rope to reach her. He gently moved her forward and motioned for her to leave the backpack. They could move faster without it. Wendy hesitated for a split second, but she knew Alex was right.

Wendy shoved her camera into her backpack. She dropped it and left everything behind. Wendy suddenly felt free. She nodded at Alex, and the two moved again as one. This crisis was over but many still lay ahead.

I'll apologize later, Wendy thought, though she knew all Alex was thinking about was reaching safety. Wendy ignored her sore ankle as burning ash hit the back of her neck, stinging like someone was tossing lit matches on her. Alex stopped suddenly at a fork in the path and Wendy bumped into him. One side was covered with trees. The other wasn't much clearer, but

Alex moved down it. They had to slow their pace to maneuver around the trees and rocks that had been tossed on the path. Neither Wendy nor Alex had time to think very clearly. They just knew they had to press on.

Wendy signaled Alex to slow down. She removed her mask and wiped it as clean as possible. Alex did the same. It did little good, as the masks almost immediately began filling again with ash. Behind them, Mount St. Helens continued to roar. Smoky had morphed into a killer. However, at least the noise seemed more distant. Maybe they'd make it after all.

But the ground beneath their feet was getting hot. Alex wondered if the soles of his boots would begin melting. Images of what was happening kept playing in Wendy's head. She was sure lava was streaming down the mountain. Would it overtake them? The ash was bad enough. Safety lay ahead, but their energy was about drained. The wind felt fiercer. Breathing remained a problem, and with each step, their lungs felt heavier and more congested.

They didn't dare stop and waste even a precious minute to put on their gloves and goggles. So their hands were burning and their eyes kept tearing. Alex had tried hiding his hands under his armpits, but it didn't work. It threw off his balance, and that was then more of a problem than burned hands. Neither dared wipe their eyes for fear that it would make their vision even worse.

Wendy yanked the rope, and Alex turned toward her. She signaled for them to stop. Both were short on breath. Alex pointed to a tall fir tree, and the two hobbled to it. They crawled under the branches and collapsed.

"We can't stay here very long," Alex warned as they again slipped on their gloves. The tree was liable to fall at any time. His voice was hoarse and rough, and his throat felt like a cat had been scratching it.

Wendy nodded, not wanting to waste her breath speaking. Although he could barely talk, Alex wanted to restore some of her confidence.

She'd need it if they were going to make it out. "You're doing great. Running track has paid off." Alex tried to make her smile. All Wendy could do was blink as she squeezed his arm. Wendy's internal clock ticked louder, and it felt like it was a time bomb ready to go off. She wondered if it would explode like Smoky. Standing, she motioned for Alex to get up. It was time to move on. With the wind continuously blowing ash, it felt like they were traveling under water.

The falling ash began to feel more like the heavy flakes in a snowstorm. *We must be near the end of the path; we have to be,* Wendy thought.

Alex urged her forward. He could detect the sounds of helicopters and trucks just ahead. The rescue missions must be set to go. They just had to reach that area. Wendy tried to picture a finish line ahead. Alex hoped his parents were waiting for him. Would he and Wendy make it?

CHAPTER 21

Alex and Wendy could barely put one foot in front of the other. Their progress had slowed to a crawl. Their breathing patterns grew shorter and shorter, and it seemed they would never reach the end of the path. *Were the sounds of the trucks and helicopters as close as they seemed?* Alex wondered. *Someday we'll laugh about this,* he thought, but without an end in sight and ash still pouring down, that seemed a long way away. Alex kept repeating to himself: *We can do this, we can do this.* He glanced back at Wendy. She limped painfully, but her face remained determined. *We'll make it,* Alex thought. He hoped Wendy could read his mind because he had no voice left. He kept spitting out ashes, which coated the inside of his throat.

Wendy barely avoided a jagged rock in the path. Unable to fully regain her breath, she wondered how much longer she could last. Her injured leg felt worse. She could barely see her boots, and when she turned around, she saw her footprints disappearing into the thick ash. *Buck up girl, you can do this,* she thought. Wendy wondered if Alex was giving himself pep talks like that. From his determined stride, Wendy was sure he was. Random thoughts kept bouncing around Wendy's head. She wondered if her photos would turn out. Images of Michael floated in and out, too. If she survived this, she would finally read a Jane Austen novel with her mother. Maybe she wouldn't even move to Iceland. One volcanic eruption was more than enough. *Focus, girl, focus.*

The earth heaved again, more trees splintered, and the two stumbled, but they caught themselves before they fell. Disaster was averted. Alex looked at Wendy, and she nodded for them to continue.

She was marshaling what felt like her last wave of energy. Hopefully it would be enough to make it to safety. Alex suddenly halted, and Wendy bumped into him.

A huge fir tree blocked their path ahead. Wendy groaned. Neither Alex nor Wendy was sure they had the strength to move any of the fallen branches. With their faces caked with ash, they looked like forlorn ghosts. They knew they couldn't climb over the obstruction. Was this the end? *Death by evergreen,* Alex thought, pushing the morbid thought away. There had to be a way around the tree. They had made it this far, and neither was ready to give up. Alex looked at one end of the tree and then at the other trying to find a solution.

Alex pointed to a small gap near one end of the fallen tree. A rock was lodged there, but they might possibly squeeze through the opening. Wendy was glad she had left her bulky backpack behind. They pulled in their stomachs and flattened themselves as much as possible and inched their way through. With his back against the rock, Alex slid through the opening. He didn't even notice that the rock shredded the back of his shirt. Wendy followed. Once free of the tree and on the path again, they gave each other a thumbs-up. Wendy was limping as much as walking, but she kept going. *I will make it. No, WE will make it,* she thought. There was no thought of stopping again. The ash storm was gaining force. Behind them, Mount St. Helens continued to explode, announcing to the world that she had finally erupted. Smoky was gone; the mountain was no longer their friend.

Suddenly, lights appeared ahead—though the flickering could be an illusion. Encouraged, Alex picked up the pace, and Wendy followed suit. The end was finally in sight. As they got closer, their thoughts turned to Michael. If he hadn't already been saved, they would have to arrange for a helicopter rescue.

Figures, human not ghostly, appeared and approached them. For a split second, Alex wondered if they were stormtroopers from a sci-fi movie who had come to take them away.

Then, he heard his name called. Still, through the curtain of ash, Alex couldn't make out who they were. But, he was so exhausted, he didn't care as long as they were there to help.

Wendy burst ahead of Alex, the rope swinging between them. *The finish line,* Wendy thought. It suddenly dawned on Alex that it was his parents calling his name. The next thing he knew, they had surrounded and embraced him and Wendy. They had made it! They were safe! Wendy's clock stopped ticking. Their seemingly endless journey was over.

Alex and Wendy were rushed to a first aid station, where a paramedic named Gail examined them. She was pleasantly surprised that the vital medical signs of the two were so strong. She told Alex's parents, "These are two resilient kids!"

Mrs. Porter applied cold compresses on their faces and gave them water to drink. She cautioned them to take little sips to prevent choking.

"We did it," Alex croaked.

"Of course, we did," Wendy managed to squeeze out. The two wanted to laugh with relief, but then they remembered Michael.

"We have to rescue Michael," Alex said. Wendy nodded, and the two stood up.

"What are you doing?" Alex's mother asked. "Sit down," Alex's father said. "Michael," was all Alex said. His parents nodded, and they all made their way to the area where the helicopters were assembled.

Gail gave the two a clean bill of health to join her and the rest of the team on the rescue mission. She was more concerned about the physical dangers involved. P.T. was more than concerned. He agreed to permit them to board but only if they remained on the craft while Pete and Gail performed the actual rescue. "It's enough that Michael knows you're on board, ready to greet him. We can't have you endangering yourselves and others by leaving the chopper."

Alex's mother signaled P.T., who turned to Alex and Wendy. "Ready to rescue Michael?"

he asked. The two nodded and boarded the helicopter. P.T. told Wendy and Alex to put on the headphones and then strap themselves in the rear seats of the converted military helicopter.

Alex's mother held her breath as the helicopter lifted off. She had promised Alex and Wendy they would rescue Michael. As the helicopter disappeared into the ash storm, she realized it was the hardest promise she ever had to keep.

"They'll be fine," Alex's father said as he squeezed his wife's hand.

"*I hope you're right,*" she thought.

CHAPTER 22

The noise of the helicopter didn't seem as unnerving to Alex as the deafening eruption a few miles away. However, he couldn't help but notice that the whir of the blades seemed erratic probably due to the ash storm. Gail, seated next to P.T., gave them the familiar "thumbs-up," so Alex relaxed a little. Wendy lacked the energy to react. Alex acknowledged Gail's gesture and then closed his eyes. Images of trees barreling down the mountain and scorched evergreens filled his head, so Alex quickly opened his eyes and looked out the window. As the chopper darted across the landscape, Alex wished he had also been rescued by air! The helicopter rocked

as it neared Michael's house. Alex told himself
it was just normal turbulence—he felt the same
sensation on a vacation flight to New York City
with his parents. However, as the helicopter kept
swaying, Alex changed his mind. He sat frozen
in his seat. He glanced at Wendy, who seemed
either lost in thought, totally exhausted, or both.

Wendy was recovering well from their ordeal
and not feeling as drained as when she first
boarded. From the air, she could see very little
through the haze of ash. *Would the ash ever
stop falling?* she wondered while reaching for
her camera to take more photos. She paused
and then remembered her camera had been left
behind. *Probably burned up by now.* Wendy
fingered the two rolls of film in her pocket. Ash
had seeped into her pockets, and the rolls of
film felt grimy and dirty. Perhaps the photos
she snapped could be saved. Alex would want
the "before" photos she had taken of Smoky.
She was surprised so little time had passed. Just
two hours ago, the sky had been a sparkling
blue and cloudless, and the mountaintop had

been covered in ice. Spirit Lake had been clear and inviting. Now, the landscape resembled a smoke-filled battleground.

The helicopter banked left, and Wendy pointed out the window. Alex spotted Michael's lodge coming into view. It was barely visible through all the ash, but Alex recognized its outline. The helicopter circled and then headed toward the small field near the house.

P.T.'s voice came over the headphones. "We're coming in as low as we can. I don't want to land because the ash is starting to clog the motor, and I'd rather keep the blades moving. We don't have much time, so Pete and Gail will find Michael and get him onboard."

As they descended the rope ladder, Wendy reminded them, "Don't forget to tell Michael we're here."

To everyone's disappointment, Pete and Gail returned several minutes later empty handed. Michael was nowhere to be found in his ruined lodge or in the immediate vicinity.

Alex asked Pete, "Did you search the shed?"

"What shed?" answered Gail.

"It's in the gully behind the lodge," Wendy said.

"We'll go back and search it," Pete responded.

"You'll never find the shed in all that ash without me."

Wendy corrected Alex. "You mean US."

P.T. wasn't comfortable sending the two kids out, but he had little choice.

Alex started to untie the rope that still bound him to Wendy, but he decided to leave it. They'd rescue Michael together. The same team that earlier had made it off the mountain would now rescue their friend. It would be one last mission on this unforgettable day.

Alex and Wendy climbed down the ladder. Once on the ground, they stumbled but popped up quickly. Both were used to the rope between them by now. Pete and Gail closely followed the pair. They passed Michael's lodge. Trees had toppled onto the porch, and the roof had collapsed. They proceeded to a spot below the rear of the lodge. Hidden by the ash was Michael's shed, still intact. They only had minutes to find Michael and get him on board.

Pete yanked the door open, and inside was Michael crouched under a tarp. He had on his goggles and mask. Even Dusty the cat wore a mask. His fur was caked with ash. It was hard to tell where the ash ended and his fur began! The rescuers would have laughed if the situation weren't so dire. Alex was so relieved that he almost burst into tears. Pete let Alex and Wendy move forward, as Michael seemed a little disoriented, and he didn't want to frighten the elderly gent. They were running out of time and had to get Michael aboard the helicopter before the ash shut down the engine.

Alex rushed to Michael and gently took his arm. Michael smiled as Alex and Wendy led him from the shed. "I knew you'd come," Michael said.

Wendy readjusted his mask. Cradled in Michael's arms was his cat who was truly dusty with a thin coating of ash on his fur. The group moved to the helicopter, where Pete jumped aboard and then reached down to help Michael climb up. Wendy, Alex, and Gail scurried into the helicopter. Immediately, the door slammed shut and P.T. took off. The engine made chugging sounds and Alex crossed his fingers, hoping that the return trip to the rescue station would be smooth. The only sound inside the helicopter was Dusty softly meowing, which was barely audible over the whirring of the chopper blades.

The helicopter shuddered and dipped, and everyone onboard held their breath, but the engine didn't die and the craft was able to ascend. Ash swirled around them, and the blades barely seemed able to cut through it. The short ride seemed to take hours. As the first aid station came into view, everyone aboard the helicopter let out a sigh of relief. The pilot finally landed the aircraft, and with the engine quieted, they all realized they were lucky to be alive. Pete helped Michael out of the helicopter and then gave Wendy and Alex a hand. Wendy was never so glad to feel earth under her feet, even if the ground was thick with ash. Alex gave Michael his cat, who was feverishly licking the ash off his fur.

Alex's parents rushed over and again hugged them. For once, Alex didn't shy away from the public display of affection. He knew at some point that Wendy would remind him and try to hug him again in public, but right now he didn't care. They had survived the eruption of Mount St. Helens, and that was all that mattered.

"Thank you," Michael murmured.

Alex and Wendy simply nodded. They were just too tired to make a sound. *That has to be a first for Wendy,* Alex thought. They slowly exited the rescue station. They wore clean masks and carried a ton of ointment to rub over their skin once they returned home. They piled into the car, but were concerned the engine wouldn't turn over. After the third try, Alex's father got out and lifted the hood, trying to wipe away as much ash as he could. Back in the car, he turned the key and the engine burst to life. It didn't sound great, but they could probably reach home.

Alex looked back at Smoky. He could barely see her through the clouds of ash and dirty windows. It was a disaster. Time would tell if it was as bad as Vesuvius or Krakatoa, but to Alex, that didn't matter. His mountain would never be the same—and neither would life around Mount St. Helens.

He could still hear trees cracking and splintering. One of the workers had said it looked like the whole mountain had been logged with huge trees just rolling down the hill. Spirit Lake was an unrecognizable mud pile. Some thought the lake had just disappeared. Within an hour of the eruption, the first of four mudflows had surged down the Toutle River. Muddy water overflowed the banks. The debris-filled waters had raged and smashed bridges, killed all wildlife in its path, and washed away homes.

The car engine conked out before it reached home. The group abandoned the car and walked the rest of the way, unsure what would await them. Wendy and Alex were still tied together. Alex's dad helped Michael along. Ash covered the house, which was dirty, but still standing. Alex's family was lucky. Trees had fallen all around their property, but none had crushed the house. They lived far enough away from the rivers that it hadn't been washed away either.

Alex and his family were relieved, although it would take them months to restore their premises. Alex wasn't sure they would ever get rid of all the ash, but thankfully all of his family were safe. "There's no place like home," Wendy muttered. And for the first time in a long time, Alex laughed. He was too tired to click his boot heels, if he even had any heels left, but they had made it.

"Home, sweet home," Alex's mother sighed as she pushed the door open.

CHAPTER 23

TWO MONTHS LATER

Wendy and her mother were due to arrive in Nighthawk that afternoon. Alex and Wendy had spoken over the phone several times, but this was her first visit since the eruption, and Alex couldn't wait.

Earlier, President Jimmy Carter visited the area to survey the damage, along with Washington Governor Dixy Lee Ray. The President told the residents he was proud of their courage and pledged to help the area rebound. Alex was in the crowd and he felt like the President was talking directly to Wendy and him about their bravery.

http://abcnews.go.com/Archives/video/22-1980-carter-visits-mt-st-helens-9624228

http://www.npr.org/templates/story/story.php?storyId=4655701

After weeks of tiring work, the Porter household had finally returned to some semblance of normalcy. There were still hidden pockets of ash around, but most of it had been cleared away. Alex had never swept, scrubbed, or polished so much in his life. Stories about the eruption abounded. Alex's parents complained that the house would never be clean enough, but that didn't bother Alex as much as it did them. *Guess that's a grown-up thing,* he thought.

Alex learned that when he and Wendy had been fleeing across the mountainside to safety, hundreds of logs were floating downstream at the time the eruption finally hit. Then the melting ice from the higher elevations of the mountain had created massive flooding. The sudden surge of water had uprooted trees, and those trees joined the logs in the rivers. Soon the waterways around the mountain were blocked by this debris, making them impassable. Shipping had been halted along the Columbia River. No large ships could pass through. The U.S. Army Corps of Engineers had to clear a path for vessels to navigate the river. It had taken over a week to dredge the path and clear the bottom of the river. Finally, river traffic could pass, and residents returned to work along the river.

One great fear was the fate of salmon and other fish. Every species in Spirit Lake perished, and ecologists were pessimistic about whether the salmon population, in particular, would ever return.

Michael, however, was optimistic. "The cycle of life continues, and it becomes richer and fuller," he said. "Mother Nature reinvents herself."

Alex wasn't sure if Michael was lying to raise his spirits or if it was really true. Alex was skeptical whether Smoky would ever fully recover, but he wanted to believe she could. He'd ask Wendy—she'd probably have an opinion. Alex did know, however, that it would take years for the area around Nighthawk to be restored.

Weeks after that initial blast, townspeople were still sweeping ash from roads and vehicles. Alex's father had installed a wraparound air filter so their car would remain running. Alex thought it looked like something out of a sci-fi movie. The ash had clogged the pipes leading into Alex's house and, for a while, his family had been without water. They felt much like nineteenth century pioneers homesteading on the prairie. No water, no electricity, and—worst of all—no television. Alex decided he really wouldn't want to live in the past. Luckily, there was enough water in Nighthawk, so even though everyone had to limit their use, Alex and his family finally had an ample supply. Alex was grateful to be able to take a shower, though he'd never admit it—especially not to Wendy.

Then there were all the reports about the long-term effects of the ash on the health and well-being of local residents. Alex couldn't wait to share them with Wendy. He hoped they could do some research on their own and figure out what was true and what was not. Even his parents didn't totally agree on the dangers of the ash. Some reports said it contained sulfuric acid and, when mixed with water, would burn skin. Alex thought that might be true since he still had to rub ointment over his skin where the ash had left burn marks. His mother, though, insisted that he would recover completely and the burn marks were from heat, not sulfur. His father, on the other hand, wasn't so sure. Alex just wanted the ash to go away. He also had marks on his back where the rock had shredded his shirt. Those, too, would fade over time. Wendy said she now had a pixie cut—whatever that was. All Alex knew was she had cut her red hair short, as a lot of it had been singed on their walk to safety. Alex was sure that no matter the style, it still would look like a bright red flame.

Like about everyone else around Nighthawk, Alex often wore a protective mask outdoors. One reason was that the volcanic ash still irritated his

217

throat. He continually wanted to scratch his nose when he was outside. At least Alex's mask was thin and looked—at least in his estimation—very cool in appearance. The police and firefighters wore bulky gas masks that looked scary. The gas masks were not very helpful because the ash clogged them. Wendy, of course, had said she had had the right type of mask. Alex hated to admit it, but she was right. Many people, including Alex's mother, now used coffee filters to make masks. This homemade version proved to be effective. Of course, the suggestion had come from Wendy, who never let Alex or anyone else forget that it was her idea.

Various methods to rid the area of the ash were tried, some rather clever. Several farmers pooled their money and hired helicopter pilots to fly over their orchards. The whir of the blades and the wind created blew the ash off the leaves and fruit. Snowplows and heavy earth-moving equipment removed truckloads of ash. Alex believed one full truckload was collected from their street alone.

Residents tried to keep a sense of humor about the ash. Alex's father said that the state of Washington should drop the *W* and thereafter be called "Ashington." Alex laughed, but his mother didn't. Handwritten signs appeared around Nighthawk. One at the town's only gas station read: *"Don't be fooled by any substitutes. Mount St. Helens ash only 50 cents a gallon, a pure ash bargain."*

The ash residue became a popular souvenir of sorts. Some people in Nighthawk tried mailing it to family and friends in other parts of the country. Workers at the post office were annoyed with "ash letters." The mailing envelopes would tend to burst, scattering ash all over the place. Artists used it to make hand-blown glass objects. Alex was given a blue globe made from the ash, which he hung in his bedroom window. It reminded him of the beauty that Smoky and Spirit Lake had been. Although Alex enjoyed the meaningful decoration, after their perilous journey through the ash, he had no desire to keep small piles of it around as mementos. Alex had ash seared in his memory, and that was about enough.

One exception was half the rope that bound him to Wendy on that trek home. Ash gray, frayed, and singed, the rope wasn't much to look at, but it meant everything to Alex and Wendy.

Alex heard the slamming of car doors from in front of his house. At last, Wendy and her mother had arrived! Mrs. Porter rushed out to greet her friend, and the two were soon chattering like the sparrows that were now being heard around Nighthawk again. Alex almost didn't recognize Wendy with her short hair, and she also seemed taller. He noticed she still favored her injured leg. During their flight, Wendy had strained her Achilles tendon, which was still healing. Wendy was wearing a coffee-filter mask that she had decorated with bright red flowers. The flowers sort of matched her hair—well, what was left of it. Wendy saw Alex staring at her hair. *Boys are so weird.* Wendy pulled off her mask. "So, like my new 'do?"

Wendy fluffed her hair and waited. She knew Alex would have no clue about how to respond.

Wendy thought Alex was *so* predictable. She put her hands under her armpits and began to crow. Alex looked really confused. "Come on, guess!" she said. "Who do I remind you of? I can fly. Come with me to Neverland, Alex."

Alex laughed. Wendy did resemble Peter Pan.

"Hey, I should be Peter Pan, since you're Wendy, one of Peter Pan's friends," Alex said.

"Get real, I'm the star," Wendy retorted. "Peter Pan has always been played by women."

Ah, Wendy and her facts, Alex thought. The two friends laughed as they went inside.

"So, I changed my mind. I'm not moving to Iceland, the center of everything volcano." Wendy announced.

"Gee, that's a surprise," Alex said, mockingly.

Wendy replied, "HA-HA, no really, I now want to be an ecologist, which means I have some good news for you!"

"Yeah, what is it? You're moving to Mars?" Alex exclaimed with a laugh.

"You're such a joker...NOT!" Wendy responded. "But seriously, I've been reading about what happens after a volcano erupts, and the good news is that nature does restore things."

"Any time table, oh wise one?" Alex asked.

"Well, it will take years for Mount St. Helens to return to her former glory, but the good news is that eventually she will," Wendy said.

Alex sat down when Wendy took a deep breath. He knew a lecture was coming, but for once he looked forward to it.

Wendy continued. "Some things worked in Smoky's favor actually limiting the damage. That spring had been late and the eruption happened early in the morning helped. Nocturnal animals were asleep deep in burrows and were protected. And because spring was late this year, deep snowbanks protected plants and animals buried beneath them. Plus, some insects were able to return to the mountain fairly quickly. Some species even survived the eruption. Some of these insects had seeds and were able to sow them. This will help the mountain recover."

"Okay. So thanks to some bugs that weren't wiped out, good old Smoky will be the same?" Alex asked.

"No, she won't be the same, but over time animals like the elk will return, and so will all the birds. Soon you'll be able to hear the birds sing, not just the sparrows. The other important thing is—you know all that ash that you hate so much?"

Alex nodded vigorously. He really did hate the ash. "Well, it turns out that it enriches the soil. So plants will grow. And so, as Michael would say, the chain of life will continue."

"I can live with that," Alex commented. "You know they had to install a pump system in Spirit Lake so she wouldn't flood the area."

"I didn't know that," Wendy replied.

"Wow, I know something you don't?" Alex taunted Wendy.

"It's just one thing, don't be a dweeb," she replied. "But all in all, it's good news."

"You're right, as usual." Alex admitted.

"I knew you'd like my news," Wendy replied. "So do you still watch *Saturday Night Live*?"

"We just got back our electricity, so I'm probably a few shows behind," Alex replied.

"Well, you've missed some good ones, let me tell you," And Wendy proceeded to tell him all about what he had missed. Alex soon concluded that the show was as funny when someone tries to explain the laughs.

Alex told Wendy the latest news about Michael who had moved to town temporarily after the eruption. He took to so-called "city life" so much that he decided to live in Nighthawk permanently. It also gave him many more opportunities to regale tourists and other outsiders with the story about his rescue from

Smoky. That story was more exciting and probably more truthful than many of the tall tales he had spun over the years.

It would be some time before Alex and Wendy hiked Smoky again, but it was comforting to know that when they did, Alex's mountain would be more like the photos Wendy had taken before the eruption and the ones frozen in his memory.

Before Wendy left for home on her first trip back to Nighthawk after the eruption, Alex presented her with a parting gift—one part of the rescue rope that he had cut in half for this occasion. He kept the other half, of course. Although the rope was parted, Alex and Wendy never have. They remain close friends to this very day.

CHAPTER 24

EPILOGUE

Over thirty years have passed since Mount St. Helens erupted on May 18, 1980 at 8:32 a.m. The mountain has recovered from that tumultuous day when ash, rock, and hot gases were spewed into the sky, followed by the deadly lava flow.

In 2004, however, many scientists and geologists wondered if the mountain was going to erupt again. Just like in 1980, volcano enthusiasts and others flocked to the mountain in anticipation of another major event. Once again, the volcano had awakened sending ash thousands of feet into the air. This activity continued for some weeks, and land near Mount

St. Helens was closed to the public. During this period, its dome was being rebuilt from magma reaching the surface of the volcano. This activity continued on and off for several years. By January 2008, the lava dome stopped growing. By July of that year, the eruptions, which had started back in 2004, finally stopped.

Today, better designed computers help monitor active volcanoes, including Mount St. Helens. Monitoring instruments fitted on lightweight stations, called "spiders" because of their spindly frames, were developed and deployed from the air by cable dangling from a helicopter. The spiders are much safer than having humans monitor the mountain, as was the case in 1980. Spiders contain equipment that measures earthquakes, ground movement, rates of lava during eruptions, and volcanic emissions. Now, supercharged spiders or so-called "smart" spiders continue to track this active volcano. The spiders are equipped to warn about likely eruptions and allow scientists to better predict when an eruption might happen, helping to save lives.

Mount St. Helens Fast Facts

- The 1980 eruption of Mount St. Helens is considered the most destructive volcanic event in U.S. history.

- Most of the structure of Mount St. Helens is fewer than 3,000 years old, meaning it is not as old as the human-made pyramids of Egypt.

- Mount St. Helens has erupted more than any other volcano in Washington's Cascade Range. Even after various eruptions, it remains an active volcano.

- About 3,600 years ago, Mount St. Helens erupted and Native Americans fled the area, which they named "Smoke Mountain."

- In 1975, geologists predicted that the mountain would erupt before the end of the century. That event occurred just five years later.

- At the time of the eruption, geologist David Johnston was tracking the mountain and radioed, *"Vancouver! Vancouver! This is it."* Those were his last public words. David Johnston died that day. Fifty-seven people were killed, including eighty-three-year-old Harry Truman, a longtime resident of the area. He owned the Mount St. Helens Lodge, which was located on Spirit Lake. He refused to evacuate, saying that he would never leave "his girl." He and his eighteen cats died that day. His remains were never found. The fictional character "Michael" in this story was inspired by Harry Truman.

Truman link: *https://www.youtube.com/watch?v=BhvfM3CNxeY*

- The ash in a huge plume rose over 80,000 feet within fifteen minutes of the eruption. The ash eventually encircled the Earth.

- By the afternoon of the 1980 eruption, the sky in the area was so dark that streetlights in nearby cities had to be turned on.

- Mudflows destroyed twenty-seven bridges and 200 homes.

- In September 2004, Mount St. Helens reawakened and erupted continuously until January 2008.

- Today, Mount St. Helens has recovered from the disaster and is a world-famous laboratory where scientists study volcanoes, the Earth's core and movements, and nature's response to volcanoes.

- Just six days after the eruption, Wendy's favorite comedienne, Gilda Radner, made her last appearance on *Saturday Night Live* (May 24, 1980).

Quick Quiz:

Choose the right answer to each question.

1. Wendy's favorite subject is:
   a. gym
   b. art
   c. English
   d. science

2. Alex is described as
   a. popular and funny
   b. a lone wolf
   c. a handsome dude
   d. quiet and timid

3. Vesuvius is
   a. an active volcano in Italy
   b. a famous Italian writer
   c. a dormant volcano in the Cascade
      Range
   d. an Italian soccer player

4. In 1980, the President of the United States was
   a. Ronald Reagan
   b. Bill Clinton
   c. Jimmy Carter
   d. George Bush

5. The fictional town nearest to Alex's home is
   a. Cascade
   b. Nighthawk
   c. Tranquility
   d. Smokyville

1. d 2. b 3. a 4. c 5. b

Sources:

http://mountsthelens.com

http://www.livescience.com/27553-mount-st-helens-eruption.html

http://pubs.usgs.gov/fs/2000/fs036-00/

http://volcanoes.usgs.gov/volcanoes/st_helens/

http://old.seattletimes.com/special/helens/timeline.html

Lauber, Patricia. *Volcano: The Eruption and Healing of Mount St. Helens.* New York: Simon and Schuster, 1993.

Parchman, Frank. *Echoes of Fury: The 1980 Eruption of Mount St. Helens and the Lives It Changed Forever.* Kenmore, Washington: Epicenter Press, Inc., 2005.

Survival is their greatest goal . . . and escaping is their only choice!

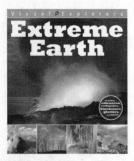

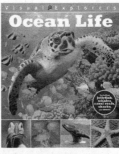
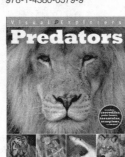